KERRIGAN

Also by James A. Ritchie

The Payback
Over on the Lonesome Side

KERRIGAN

James A. Ritchie

Walker and Company
New York

First published in the United States of America in 1993 by Walker
Publishing Company, Inc.

Published simultaneously in Canada by Thomas Allen & Son Canada,
Limited, Markham, Ontario

Library of Congress Cataloging-in-Publication Data
Ritchie, James A.
Kerrigan / James A. Ritchie.
p. cm.
ISBN 0-8027-1276-2
I. Title.
PS3568.I814K47   1993
813'.54—dc20   93-8065
CIP

Printed in the United States of America

2   4   6   8   10   9   7   5   3   1

TO LAWRENCE BLOCK for help he probably doesn't remember giving. To Louis L'Amour who said it better than I ever can. To Uncle Jack for letting me live the life for a few years. And as always, to those who have loved me enough to be there even when I'm too often wrong.

AUTHOR'S NOTE

MANY OF THE CHARACTERS in this novel are actual historical figures, but one, Lynn Smith, is of particular interest to me. In a reference to him that I came across while researching this novel I learned that he lived in my home town of New Castle, Indiana, and seems to have played an important role in Alaska's early history. Since New Castle even now has a population of only sixteen thousand, learning of Lynn Smith was a pleasant surprise.

I would, however, like to know much more about him than I've been able to learn. Anyone knowing anything about him may write to me at the following address: James A. Ritchie, 91 Stonegate Dr., New Castle, IN 47362.

KERRIGAN

CHAPTER 1

I WAS TIRED of running, tired of always looking over my shoulder in an effort to stay one step ahead of Thornton's men. I was weary of the cold, lonesome trails and the one-horse towns where I dared not stop for more than a few days at a time. In my weariness, I let myself believe that Fergus Thornton had given up trying to find me.

Some wiser voice in the back of my mind told me he wasn't the kind of man who would quit, that he had lost two sons at my hands and would not rest until one of us was dead. That was what my inner voice told me, but after a time I ignored the voice and began looking for a place to settle down. I found it when I rode onto a small ranch only fifty miles from Cheyenne. Right from the start, it felt like home.

Yet even as I was certain I'd found the perfect place to stop and build a life, Fergus Thornton was always in the back of my mind.

It had begun just over a year earlier. I was riding the grub line in Texas, looking for any kind of work a man could do from the hurricane deck of a cow pony, when I came across the herd Fergus Thornton and his brood of four sons were just starting up the trail to market. They needed men and I needed work, so I signed on.

For a time all went smoothly, and while Fergus Thornton was a man willing to work those under him half to death, he always put in as many hours, and often more. That's the kind of boss a man doesn't mind working for.

Fergus was a big man who came over from Ireland while still in his twenties, and in the thirty years since, he'd built one of the biggest and best ranches in Texas. At fifty-five, his red hair was well sprinkled with gray, and the weathered lines on his face told a hard story. But he was still the old bull of the woods.

All his sons were born in Texas, and they were as alike, and as different, as brothers can be. But Fergus and his sons had one thing in common . . . they were all fighting men. Fergus raised his sons by the law of the feud and the belief that nothing was more important than family.

Me, I had two brothers out wandering about the country, but we Kerrigans are an independent lot. Each of us straddled a horse and went his own way the moment we were old enough to get by in the world. I hadn't heard from either of my brothers in almost four years, not since Pa died, and somehow it seemed natural.

It wasn't that we didn't care for each other, but like I said, we Kerrigans like to go our own way.

But I have to admit, I envied the way Fergus Thornton and his sons rode together, worked together, and fought together. It was a fine thing to see, and sometimes made me wish my own family felt the same.

Roland Thornton was the eldest of Fergus's sons, and of them all, he was the one I didn't particularly like. He wore a matched set of ivory-handled Colts, and he wore them tied down. Roland was always riding away from the herd to practice with those Colts, and most of his talk was about some gunfighter or another he'd heard stories about.

Now, I've never been a gunfighter as such. I mean, I've had gun trouble a time or two, but I never hired out my gun. Though I did have a reputation in parts of New Mexico and Arizona, I wasn't proud of it. So I tried talking to Roland, tried to tell him what a gunfight was really like.

I told him someone almost always dies, and how ugly it is to put a bullet in a man and watch him bleed and die with his face in the dirt and fear in his eyes. I also told him the man dying could easily be you, because there's always somebody better . . . or luckier.

Roland didn't buy anything I was trying to sell. He kept practicing his fast draw, and he was itching for a chance to use his Colts against something other than tin cans and jackrabbits.

Then the herd passed within a few miles of a two-by-twice town just large enough to have a saloon. Fergus allowed it wouldn't hurt to ride in and wash the trail dust from our throats, so leaving three men to watch the cattle, the rest of us rode in for a drink and a hot meal.

Only four men were in the saloon when we entered, but one of those men was young and wore an old Colt. Roland took one look at him and I smelled trouble. It wasn't long in coming.

With a couple of beers and a plate of hot food in his belly, Roland looked around for some way of entertaining himself. His eyes landed on the stranger with the Colt. Roland began taunting the fellow, and I could see anger in the man's eyes.

But to his credit, he quickly finished his drink and started out of the saloon, not wanting trouble with Roland or anyone else. Only he had to pass right by Roland's table to reach the door, and as he did Roland stuck out his foot and tripped him.

That was the final straw. The man came to his feet, anger all over him, and he drew. Now, the plain truth is that Roland wasn't all that fast, but he'd put in enough practice to be better than the average cowboy, so he put two bullets in the man's chest without any trouble. Then he watched the man die, and he smiled.

The town was small enough not to have a sheriff, but it probably wouldn't have mattered. In my mind what Roland did was murder, but the other man drew first, and that would be all that counted with the law.

We rode back to the herd, and from that moment on,

Roland was on the prod. Killing that cowboy was all he talked about, and after a few days I'd heard all I wanted to hear. The third night out of town, we were sitting around the fire, eating beef and beans, when Roland started bragging again about the killing.

He made it about halfway through his story, then looked at me. "Go ahead and tell them," he said. "You were there. Tell these boys about it."

I couldn't think of anything to say that might not start a fight, so I stood up and started to walk away, thinking to eat alone. Roland came to his feet.

"Where do you think you're going?" he asked. "I told you to tell them about the gunfight."

"Most of us were there," I said, "and you've told the others about it a dozen times already. You don't need my help."

"It ain't polite to walk away from a man when he's talking to you," Roland said. "I don't like it."

I sighed. "Look, I'm not trying to start a fight. All I want to do is walk over there by that log and eat in private."

"You want to go over there and eat, go ahead. But you'll have to crawl."

"Let it drop, Roland. It isn't worth fighting about."

He laughed. "I think you're yellow, Kerrigan. So either sit down here and do like you were told, or crawl over to that log."

Some things a man can't take, and being called a coward is one of them. Times being what they were, something like that could follow a man for life. In a land like that, a man's life often depended on those around him, how they would react if trouble came. If I let Roland call me a coward I'd never find work on another ranch, and not a man anywhere would trust me.

My plate was in my left hand, and a cup of coffee was in my right. I turned to face Roland, but I didn't empty my hands. "Roland," I said, "I've seen you draw. You're decent for a cowhand, but that's all. If you draw on me I'll kill you."

Fergus Thornton was near the fire, and so were his sons and four other men. Fergus was a man who'd been there and back, and I think he saw the truth in my eyes.

"Tell him, Fergus," I said. "Talk some sense into him."

He looked at Roland, then back at me. He dropped his eyes when he spoke. "It's his fight, Kerrigan. I can't tell him to back down."

I nodded. "All right, Roland," I said. "It's your play. Let it drop and we'll both forget it ever happened. Or you can draw and I'll kill you. Your choice."

Fergus Thornton's youngest son, Trace, was right there watching it happen. Of them all, he was the one I'd been friendliest with, and more than once we'd ridden out to scout the trail together. On one of those rides a rattlesnake frightened his horse and I killed it, drawing and shooting the snake's head off from twenty yards.

Trace was only seventeen, but he was man enough to speak his piece. "Don't do it, Rolly. I've seen Kerrigan shoot, and he's fast. His hand was a blur. He'll kill you for sure."

"Him kill me? He never saw the day."

And just like that he drew. His hand was near the butt of his Colt, and he drew without warning. Dropping the coffee cup, I snapped my Colt from the holster. His pistol was coming into line when I fired. My first bullet hit the third button up on Roland's shirt, and the second bullet wasn't more than an inch higher.

The Colt fell from his hand and he touched his chest almost gently. His hand came away covered with blood and his eyes went wide at the sight of it. Then he folded and fell, his head landing in the fire. Fergus roared like an old bull and grabbed Roland, pulling him from the flames. It was too late to matter. Roland was dead.

For a moment I thought Fergus was going to grab for

his own gun, but mine was still out and cocked. "Don't do it, Fergus. All of you sit quiet."

Jesse Thornton, next oldest to Roland, was sometimes a hothead, but Daniel Thornton was the one I watched closest. He was usually a quiet man, but wore a Colt like he knew how to use it; I had a hunch he might be as good as Roland had thought himself. Neither of them tried anything.

The faces around the fire displayed grief, anger, and shock. "I'm sorry," I said. "He left me no choice."

Fergus was cradling Roland's body in his arms, and when he looked up at me his face seemed to have aged. "Ride out, Kerrigan, while you can. When the burying and the mourning are done, we'll be coming for you. If I have to hire every man who can hold a gun, I'll find you and see you dead. Choice or no, you killed my son, and I won't rest until you're dead."

In another hour it would have been my turn to ride night guard, so my horse was already saddled. I stepped into the saddle, my Colt still out. "He forced the fight on me," I said. "Let it go, Fergus. I didn't want to kill him."

Fergus said nothing. I rode away from the camp and kept riding through the night and into the next morning. My hope was that Fergus would grieve for a time, then realize nothing would be gained by coming after me. But it wasn't to be. A month later a man tried to knock me from the saddle with a Sharps buffalo rifle, only he shot too fast and missed.

Diving out of the saddle and into the brush, I worked my way around and came at the man from behind. He tried to whirl and fire, but the big rifle was too heavy and too slow. My bullet burned a path across his shoulder and he dropped the rifle, cursing like a sailor.

"Why'd you take a shot at me?" I asked. "I don't recall ever seeing you before."

"Hell, man," he said. "It's nothing personal. I'm a poor

man and that reward on your head was too good to let pass."

"What reward?"

"You mean you don't know? Some fellow named Thornton wants you dead. He passed the word along that he'll pay two thousand for your scalp."

"A dead man can't spend money," I said. "If I ever see you again I'll shoot on sight."

"You're lettin' me go?"

"Leave your rifle where it is and ride out before I change my mind."

"That rifle cost a pretty penny. I'd hate to lose it."

"You can come back for it later if you want to take the chance," I said. "But you'd better be sure I'm long gone."

He took off in one direction and I went the other. It was in my mind to ride back and settle things with Fergus Thornton, but I knew that was a losing game. He had too many men and I wouldn't be able to get close. So I headed north, out of Texas, and went to wandering. Over the next twelve months two other men tried to kill me, one of them Jesse Thornton.

He caught up with me in Dodge, and he nearly did the job. He came out of the shadows with a shotgun and knocked my leg from under me with the first barrel. His second shot crossed my own, and two more buckshot caught me in the arm.

But I heard him scream and knew my bullet had found its mark. Then the marshal and a sizable crowd of spectators poured into the street and it was all over. My wounds hurt, but they weren't serious, and I was able to leave Dodge two days later.

Jesse Thornton wasn't so lucky. My bullet caught him in the stomach, and that's a hard, painful way to die.

When I left Dodge I headed west and kept out of sight, riding the wildest, high-lonesome country I could find. My right name is Clay Kerrigan, but from the moment I left Dodge I started calling myself Brent Griffin.

No more trouble came my way, and it began to look as if I'd left the trouble behind me.

By that time I'd seen more country than I ever expected to cover. My wandering stopped in Wyoming, at a small ranch fifty miles north of Cheyenne, shoved right up against the Laramie Mountains. Only a few years earlier it had all been Indian country, but the fighting was long since over and ranchers had moved in. It was wild and beautiful country, the kind of place where a man might lose himself.

I rode into a small town called Slater that sat against Chugwater Creek, wanting no more than a meal I hadn't cooked myself and maybe a night in a soft bed. I was stepping along the boardwalk, watching the hustle and bustle going on around me and not paying attention to where I was going.

As I walked past a dress shop, the door opened and a woman came out, loaded to the gills with packages.

But like I said, I wasn't paying attention to where I was going, and I didn't see her until we collided head on. Thing is, she couldn't have weighed more than a hundred and twenty, so I had a good seventy pounds on her. I staggered back a step or two, but she came off her feet and landed square on her bottom.

Those packages flew in all directions, and I started grabbing for them, trying to stammer out an apology. Then I looked right at the woman and all of a sudden I forgot who I was and what I was doing. She looked to be about nineteen, and I'd never seen anyone half as pretty.

Her hair was the color of ripe wheat on a sunny day, and her eyes were blue as the summer sky. She was wearing a lavender dress that set off her eyes and hair, and all I could do was stare.

The expression on her face was one of puzzlement, but

that quickly changed to anger. "What are you staring at?" she asked. "First you knock me down, and now you're standing there staring at me like some kind of idiot. The least you could do is close your mouth and help me up."

I realized that I was staring, and that my mouth was hanging wide open. Blood rushed to my face.

"Yes, ma'am," I said. "I sure am sorry, ma'am."

I was already holding two of her packages in my right hand, so I reached with my left to help her up. That was a mistake. Somehow we didn't get our grip quite right, and when she was halfway to her feet our fingers slipped apart and she fell again.

That made me stagger backward to catch my balance, and I accidentally stepped on one of her packages. In trying to keep my full weight from coming down on it I did a little dance, and my spur caught in the boardwalk. I fell, landing hard enough on my bottom to snap my teeth together.

The look of puzzlement was back on the woman's face, and I was pretty sure I looked the same. For a few seconds we sat there staring at each other, then she started to laugh.

I opened my mouth to ask what was so funny. Then I realized a dozen or more people were standing around watching us, and every one of them wore a big smile. I couldn't help it—I started laughing, too.

CHAPTER 2

WHEN THE LAUGHTER finally died, I tried again to help the lady up, and this time we made it. We gathered her packages, and I spent the whole time apologizing over and over.

"It's all right," she said. "In fact, it was worth getting knocked down. I haven't laughed so hard in months."

"Neither have I. I guess it was funny. Look, the least I can do is help you carry all these things, ma'am."

"My name is Angela Douglas," she said, "but everybody calls me Angie. I'm staying at the hotel with my father for the night, and I guess I could use some help. Thank you, Mr.—?"

"Brent Griffin. Let's see if we can reach the hotel without falling down, Angie."

"It won't be half as much fun, but we can try."

We reached the hotel without incident, and the moment we entered the lobby Angie ran over to a tall, slender, well-dressed man of about fifty. She pulled him over to where I stood and introduced us. Vance Douglas was wearing a gray suit with a white shirt and a string tie, but his hands and face had the tanned, weathered appearance of a man who spent most of his time outdoors. He looked fine in the suit, but out of place.

We shook hands after a bellhop took Angie's packages from me and trotted up the stairs with them. Angie told her father how we met, and he laughed. We talked for a minute, then he asked if I was in town on business.

"I guess you could say I'm looking for business," I said.

"I've spent the last year wandering around, and now I'm looking for a job."

"You've been looking for another hand, Dad," Angie said. "What about Brent?"

"I do need someone," he said. "I need a man who knows cattle, but we raise crops as well, and there's always keep-up work to be done. Everybody lends a hand when it comes to mending fences and the like. Do you know much about work like that, Mr. Griffin?"

"Yes, sir. I grew up on a hillside farm in Kentucky, so working with my hands never scared me. And I know cattle as well as most. I've worked on several ranches, and I've been on half a dozen cattle drives."

"I have a working ranch, Mr.—ah, can I call you Brent?" I nodded. "Well, Brent, as I said, I have a working ranch and we don't get into town often except for church or supplies, but this time we came in for the weekend. We'll be leaving tomorrow evening. If you're interested in the job you can ride out with us and have a look around. If you like what you see, we'll give it a try. I pay forty a month and found. Not too many pay better."

"That's sounds fine," I said. "Where can we meet?"

"Right here, about four tomorrow evening."

"Why don't you come to church with us?" Angie asked. "We're having a picnic after the service."

"That's a good idea," Vance said. "Pastor Mullen will talk your head off, but it's worth it for the food. Angie always brings enough to feed a cavalry troop."

"I'd like that," I said. "But I wouldn't want to intrude on your Sunday."

"Nonsense," Vance said. "You'll be more than welcome. It's the Baptist church right down the street. Service starts at nine."

We talked for a few more minutes, then went our separate ways. Only after leaving them did I realize how much going to church and the picnic would cost me. I had the clothes on my back, plus two old shirts and a change of jeans in my blanket roll. Nothing I owned was fit for church, but I did have a few dollars in my pocket, saved from odd jobs over the last year. It wasn't much, but it was enough.

I hunted a mercantile and bought myself a black, pin-striped suit jacket and matching pants. I also bought a white shirt and a vest. They threw in a string tie for free. My hat was battered and stained from the trail, so I bought a new Stetson as well.

A new pair of boots would have topped things off just right, but I couldn't afford anything they had. I took the clothes down to the barbershop and, after a bath and shave, tried them on. They fit, but I felt a little bit like a monkey wearing silk.

If the job with Vance Douglas didn't work out I was in trouble, because once I paid for a night in the hotel and a decent meal I'd be lucky to have two silver dollars to rub together.

They gave me a room on the top floor of the hotel, but though I came and went a good bit that evening, I didn't see Angie again. As usual, I was up early next morning. I washed up, then scraped the night's growth of whiskers off my face. I ran into Angie and Vance as I was leaving the hotel. We walked to the church together.

When I was growing up back in Kentucky, everybody would be in church come Sunday. Going to meeting, we called it, so I knew my way around. The minister opened the service with a prayer, and then we spent twenty minutes singing hymns.

I was never much on singing, but I did my best and hoped no one could tell where the sour notes were coming from. Angie stood by my side as we sang, and I held the hymn book for her. Angie's voice was a fine thing to hear, and after a time I stopped singing and listened to her.

Standing about six feet tall and weighing something like

two-thirty, Pastor Mullen was a good-sized man. When he started preaching he put everything he had into it, and he didn't let up for an hour and a half. When he spoke of hellfire I could feel the heat right through the soles of my boots.

After the preaching came the altar call, and half a dozen folks went up and knelt before the altar while the rest of us sang another hymn. When the service was dismissed there was a brief time of going around and meeting people before we left for the picnic grounds.

We walked back to the hotel first so Angie could change her dress and retrieve her picnic basket from the hotel kitchen. When she was ready, we rode to the picnic grounds in a carriage. The picnic basket sat right behind me, and before we reached the spot we were headed for, I knew most of what awaited us in the basket just by the aromas floating around me.

Vance hadn't exaggerated when he said Angie usually brought enough food to feed a cavalry troop. She had fried chicken, smoked ham, biscuits, jam, potato salad, deviled eggs, and blackberry pie. I did my best to make sure the basket would be lighter going back to town than it had been coming out.

Nothing in my life ever came easy. Growing up on a hillside farm that had more rocks than dirt made for a hard living, and keeping the wolf from the door was sometimes a close thing. Even when I left home things didn't get much better. A cowboy's life is brutal work, lonesome camps, and low pay. There's two dozen ways a man can get himself killed on a trail drive, and I've seen most of them.

Then came the trouble with Fergus Thornton and the price he had placed on my head.

Not that I was complaining. My life had been hard and lonely, but in many ways it was good. Sitting there with Angie, however, looking into the blue of her eyes, watching the way she smiled, listening to her talk, it came to me just how much I'd missed.

The picnic ended all too soon and we headed back into town. Vance took care of getting their things from the hotel while I went about my own business. There wasn't much to do, really. Changing back into my range clothing, I put just about everything I owned into my saddlebags and blanket roll, then walked down to the livery.

Instead of riding my horse, Apache, and following the carriage, I tied him behind and sat next to Angie while Vance drove. It was a bit more than two hours to the Douglas ranch, and a fine ride it was.

Fergus Thornton never once left the back of my mind, but it had been a long time since anyone tried to collect the reward, and it seemed he'd lost my trail for good. I had a new name, a new start, and it was time to begin building a life for myself.

It came to me that I was fooling myself, but all this was in my mind as I rode along beside Angie. Then I saw the ranch and I fell in love.

Vance Douglas was a rancher, but he was also something of a farmer, and a builder with an eye on the future. Only a few ranchers grew hay in any quantity, but Vance had acre after acre of the finest hay I'd ever seen. He also had a wheat field, a garden large enough to produce vegetables for the entire winter, and he was raising nearly fifty hogs and two hundred chickens.

This set Vance well apart from many of the ranchers I'd known. Most ranchers were cattle-minded to a fault, and while a few men might cut a little wild grass for hay, almost none set aside land to plant hay. And while many raised a pig or two for food and most planted a small garden, almost none did so to the extent of Vance Douglas.

When we reached the main ranch house, I realized what kind of builder Vance was. The house had two stories and was timber framed. It takes a lot of work and know-how to frame a house with timber, but it's well worth it if done right, and this one was done right. I commented on the house and Vance smiled. "I built it myself," he said. "Though I did have the help of several Indians, who provided most of the muscle.

"It was Angie's mother who wanted to come out here in the first place, if you can believe it. She knew I'd never be happy working for her father back in Illinois, and she knew I wanted to own a ranch someday, so when she heard about this land she practically dragged me out here by my heels.

"There never has been and never will be another woman like Jenny. Not unless it's Angie. You should have met her, Brent. You would have liked her."

Sometimes there's no easy way of asking a question. "She's dead?"

Vance nodded. "Cholera," he said. "It's been almost five years now."

"I'm sorry."

"I miss her," he said. "I built this home for Jenny, and it seems empty without her. But she gave me more love in the years we had together than most men could find in three lifetimes."

"I wish I could have met her," I said. "She sounds like quite a lady."

"Yes. She was that."

After twenty years, Vance Douglas was still slowly building and expanding. It wasn't yet a large ranch, but it wasn't tiny either. He had two full-time riders working for him, along with a cook and an old man who cared for the garden and did odd jobs.

The bunkhouse was large enough to hold the dozen men he needed at roundup and harvest. The ranch had all the signs of growth, and Vance hadn't overextended himself at any point.

Vance and Angie both climbed from the carriage at the

front porch, and I went to put the team and carriage away. "Come back to the house when you're done," he said.

I hate seeing good horses treated poorly, so I took my time putting those away. Once in the stable, I wiped both horses down and spent several minutes running a curry comb through their damp hair. Then I gave each horse a bucket of grain and sprinkled fresh straw on the floor of their stalls.

When I got back to the house, I knocked and Vance yelled for me to come in. The house was even prettier inside than out.

Paintings hung on some of the walls, and the rugs, curtains, and bric-a-brac showed that whoever decorated the house had an eye for beauty. The Douglas home wasn't that of a rich person, but of someone who knew and appreciated comfort and good taste.

Me, I'd never had much of anything to call my own, nor did any of my family. In Kentucky, home was a two-room cabin Pa built before I was born. It was warm and it kept the rain out, but that was about all you could say for it. And what little furniture we had was either homemade or bartered from a traveling man who sometimes had an old chair or the like on his wagon.

But a time or two I'd been in places almost as nice as the Douglas home, and each time I came away filled with longing. Someday I wanted such a place to call my own, and I wanted someone to share it with. Not that I would ever have it, not on cowboy pay, but I wanted it.

Following Vance's voice, I found myself in the kitchen. He motioned for me to sit down at the table. He poured two cups of coffee and sat down across from me, sliding a cup to me. I sipped the coffee. It was blacker than a moonless midnight, stronger than a mossback bull, and hotter than the sunny side of hell. It was cowboy coffee.

"Brent," he said, "I told you I wanted a man who could and would work with his hands, and I meant it. But if you have as much experience with cattle as you claim, and I don't doubt your word, I'd like you to spend a few days riding the range.

"It seems to me we can kill a flock of birds with one stone. You'll learn the lay of the land, you'll meet some of my neighbors, and I'll find out how well my cattle are doing. That all right with you?"

"Sure. It makes sense. When do I start?"

"Get settled in tonight, meet the other men, and start in the morning."

We spent another hour talking, and Vance laid out the boundaries of his range for me, told me where the cattle liked to drift this time of year, then threw out a bit about some of his neighbors. In particular, he told me about a man named Charlie Slaughter.

"He's a man worth meeting," Vance said. "He just came in a couple of years ago. I'd guess he's sixty-five or better, but he's nail hard and rawhide tough. He has several hundred cattle and he started with almost nothing.

"Charlie spent most of his life wandering about and was never in one place for long. But he does have a daughter back East, and he started the ranch because she needed help. He's older than some of the hills around here, but you'd never in a million years guess what he's talking about doing next."

"What's that?"

"You know where Alaska is?"

"Sure. North and west. The papers are full of stories about the gold they're finding up there."

Vance nodded. "It's north and west, all right. About three thousand miles north and west. Just to get there you have to go all the way to the West Coast, then risk your life on a ship for another thousand miles. And from what I understand, things only get worse once you're there. And you know what old Charlie Slaughter wants to do? He wants to make a trail drive to Alaska! And doggone me if I don't half believe he'll try it one of these days."

"Sounds like quite a trip," I said. "I'll have to ask him about it."

"You won't have to ask. It's all Charlie talks about. But I'll say this—Charlie has been places and done things most men wouldn't believe. Personally, I don't think anyone could make a drive like that, but if it could be done, he's the one to do it."

When we were through talking I went out to the bunkhouse and stowed my gear. I hadn't stabled Apache, thinking I might need him before the evening was over, but once my gear was stowed, I stripped off his saddle, and let him into the corral. I brought him an armload of hay and a bit of grain, then pumped more water into a trough inside the corral.

There was no one around, so I took a walk, wanting to look things over. Walking is something I've always enjoyed, and I must have covered a couple of miles before turning around and heading back. It was close to dark, but as I walked past the barn I heard the sound of a hammer inside. Going in, I found an old man trying to hold a long plank against the wall with one hand, and trying to get a nail in with the other. He was having trouble.

Coming up from behind him, I grabbed the plank just as it slipped from his hand. "You look like a man who's a hand short," I said. "You want to hammer or hold?"

He grinned. "Guess I'll hammer. I've been wrestling these things most of the afternoon. Gets to be work after a while. You hire on with Vance?"

"Today. My name is Brent Griffin."

"Caleb McEntire."

The barn was long, wide, and high. Caleb was adding a room to the inside rear of the barn. He had the floor down, and now it was a matter of adding two walls, a door, and a window. The job was half complete, and the work he'd done was excellent, with no gaps in the joints, the framing straight and solid. "You're a hand with tools," I said. "You must enjoy building."

"Been at it close to sixty years," he said. "Sometimes it feels like I've put up half the buildings in the country, but I do enjoy it, for a fact. At my age, though, little jobs like this are plenty. And when my bones get tired of this, I go work in the garden. But this is why I don't retire to a rocker."

"Have you been with Vance long?"

"About ten years. I'm seventy years old, and I reckon this will be my last job on earth. If it is, I'm glad it's with Vance. Never had a better boss."

"He seems like a good man," I said.

Caleb banged another nail home and grinned. "He is, but I'll bet it don't hurt that his daughter is such a filly. We get about a dozen young bucks a month coming through asking for work, all because of Miss Angie. Usually Vance sends 'em packing."

"It was Angie who asked Vance to hire me."

"Do tell? Might be you've got the inside track, then. If you have, don't let it go to your head. There's fifty men around these parts who would ride through hell to get at the man who hurts Angie. It's really none of my business, and I hope you take no offense. Just telling you how she stands, is all."

"No offense taken," I said. "Besides, I'm just a wandering cowboy. It isn't likely someone like Angie would look at me twice."

"Maybe, and maybe not," Caleb said. "There's no figuring what a woman will do or why she'll do it. And Miss Angie is sure enough a woman."

"Yes, sir," I said. "She is that."

We worked another twenty minutes, then Caleb laid down his hammer and stretched his arms.

"Snakepot will have grub ready by now," he said. "We'd best go on in before he throws it away."

"Snakepot?"

Caleb shrugged. "His rightful name is Willard. Willard Campbell. The way I heard it, he was cook on a trail drive several years back, and he served rattlesnake stew near every day. The boys took to calling him Snakepot, and the name stuck."

"I've eaten rattlesnake a few times," I said. "It beats some meals I've had."

The bunkhouse had a kitchen built onto the back, and we washed up at a basin near the door. Two cowboys were sitting at a long table when we went inside. One was slim, red-haired, and couldn't have been more than eighteen. The other was tall, wide, and balding. His eyes reminded me of an old hound dog. Caleb introduced the redhead as Ted Kitchell, and the balding man as Jules Wisehart. I shook hands with them both.

About then, a man came through a door on the far side of the room, carrying a large kettle in one hand and a pan of cornbread in the other.

"What'd you fix us tonight, Snakepot?" Jules asked. "More of them Mexican firecrackers, I'll bet."

Snakepot was somewhere near fifty, and not much above the five-foot mark. He wore a two- or three-day growth of whiskers, and his apron carried food stains from several past meals.

"What else?" Snakepot growled. "Any man complains about beans and cornbread around here will be whinin' all the time."

"Now that's the gospel truth," Jules said. "I'm about ready to try some of that snake stew you're so famous for, Snakepot. At least that would be a change."

Snakepot grunted and went back out the door into the kitchen area. When he was gone, Ted smiled. "Don't let Jules fool you," he said to me. "Snakepot ain't the cleanest man I've ever known, but he can cook. It's true enough we have beans and cornbread most nights, but it don't usually stop there. Wait and see."

Ted was right. In the time it took us to fill our plates with beans and cornbread, Snakepot had brought out mashed potatoes, green beans, a platter of sliced ham, and a bowl of gravy. I'm an eating man from way back and did justice to what was served.

Snakepot kept the coffee coming as well, and just when it looked like the meal was over he carried in a fresh-baked blackberry pie. It was a big pie, but the four of us put it away in nothing flat.

When the last speck of pie was scraped from my plate, I leaned back with a cup of coffee and groaned. Snakepot came in to clear the table and I caught his eye. "Snakepot," I said, "I don't know what you're being paid, but it's not enough. I've never eaten better."

Snakepot looked at Jules. "Leastways we got one man around here who knows good when it hits his tongue. 'Bout time the boss hired someone with sense."

"Ah, Snakepot," Jules said. "You know I was just funnin' with you."

"Be that as it may," Snakepot said. "You keep it up and one day you'll wish I would serve up a pot of snake."

"What does that mean?"

"Keep it up and you'll find out."

Supper over, we left the kitchen and went back to the bunkhouse. The kitchen was built onto the bunkhouse, but you had to go outside to get from one to the other. The night was cool, and after the heat of the kitchen it felt good. A shooting star darted across the sky, and for a moment we all stopped and watched. Not one of us said a word, but I think we all made a secret wish.

In the bunkhouse, I pulled off my boots, hung my gun belt next to my bunk, and stretched out. We talked for a time, but work starts early and ends late on a ranch, so it wasn't long before Ted blew out the lamp. Minutes later we were all asleep.

CHAPTER 3

NO MATTER WHAT time I get to sleep I can't seem to keep at it once the sun comes up. The others were still snoring when I eased into my clothes, strapped on my Colt, and went outside. It was late August, but the sun was no more than halfway above the horizon, and there was a chilly nip to the morning air. A light, wispy fog hung over the fields, and the grass was heavy with dew. A rooster crowed nearby and a second answered.

Rolling a smoke, I touched a match to it and walked around to the kitchen, hoping Snakepot would be awake and starting breakfast. He was awake, but the only thing he had on the stove was coffee. That was fine by me.

"Those other three'll sleep awhile yet," he said. "What roused you so early?"

"Habit. Been getting up early since I was old enough to wear long pants. And I kind of like the morning, when you get down to it."

"Well, there's coffee, and you're welcome to it, but it'll take a spell for food. Stove ain't been hot long."

"Coffee's fine," I said. "Vance wants me to take a few days to ride around and learn the ranch. No sense putting it off until the day's half over."

Snakepot disappeared through the door leading to the stove, returned with a big cup of coffee.

"If you want to wait," he said, "I can at least fry a few eggs. Won't take a minute."

"Sounds good. Thanks. Who do I see about range grub? I'll be gone two or three days, maybe more."

"I'm the one to see about any kind of food on this

ranch," he said. "Miss Angie is a fine cook, taught her myself, but the boss eats out here with us half the time. He's a good man, Vance Douglas is. Good as any I ever worked for, and better than most."

"Seems like."

"None of my business," Snakepot said, "but what brings a man like you this way? I mean, this place is mighty nice, but it's small and in the middle of nowhere."

I sipped my coffee. "What do you mean, a man like me? I'm a cowhand like any other."

"Maybe. But you wear that Colt like a man who's real comfortable with it. In fact, I bet you'd look naked without it. No matter how you move around, your right hand never gets far from the holster. Just look at yourself. Even sittin' there drinkin' coffee that right hand never gets any rest. I may be a cranky old man, but I've been up the trail and back, Griffin. I've seen the old gunfighters, and you'd fit right in with the crowd."

"Snakepot, I said I'm a hired hand, and I meant it. Let's just say I've been up the trail and back myself, and let it go at that."

"Fair enough. Nothing agin you, Griffin. It's only that I'd hate to see trouble come to this ranch. I like the boss, and Miss Angie is real special."

"That's straight talk, Snakepot, so I'll return it. I have used a Colt, and I've ridden some hard trails, but if there's trouble it'll have to come looking for me. All I want is a day's pay for a day's work. And I want to be left alone."

For a time he looked at me. Then he rubbed his chin whiskers and nodded. "I believe you, Griffin. I hope you took no offense at me buttin' into your business. Like I said, I'm a cranky old man. Guess I don't worry about bein' polite."

"No offense taken, Snakepot. In your place I'd have done the same thing, like as not."

"In that case, I'll get to work on those eggs and pack the grub you'll need for your ride. Won't take long."

Snakepot was true to his word. In five minutes he had a plate of eggs sitting in front of me, along with a large chunk of day-old bread to sop the yolks. As I finished the eggs, Snakepot brought out a gunnysack stuffed with food.

"That should hold you a few days," he said. "You got cookin' ware?"

"A skillet and a coffeepot. I'll make do."

Draining the last of the coffee from my cup, I stood up and went outside, carrying the sack of food. Ted, Jules, and Caleb were just coming out of the bunkhouse. Caleb looked ready to start a day's work, but Ted and Jules were both bleary-eyed and a bit unsteady. "You boys may as well go back to sleep," I said. "The day is half over and I've done all the work."

Jules mumbled something unkind about early risers, and Ted grunted. Caleb winked. "They're good boys," he said. "If you can get 'em awake. First time in a coon's age I recall anyone gettin' out of bed before me. Guess I'm gettin' old."

"If I could get the hang of it," I said, "I'd sleep late every morning. My pa used to say a man had to get up before the sun if he wanted to amount to anything."

"Was he right?"

"Too soon to tell. I keep hoping."

I went to the corral, hung the sack on a fence post and saddled Apache, then climbed on his back. For a moment he stood firm and I waited, knowing what was coming. His muscles suddenly tightened under me and he went to bucking. We went around the corral twice, then he stopped as suddenly as he started.

Apache was a mustang and still half wild, but that was the kind of horse I wanted under me if trouble came. He wouldn't buck the rest of the day. He might even let several mornings slip by without putting up a fight.

Snatching the sack of food from the fence post, I reached around and tied it to my saddlebags. Then I pointed Apache northwest and rode out. The sun was still not far above the horizon, a red ball bathing the landscape with pale light. We rode through belly-high grass, and in spots I could still see traces of fog.

What more could any man ask than a morning like that and the chance to ride free across the land?

It was beautiful country, and I spent most of two days riding across it and counting cattle before stopping in to see any of Vance's neighbors for more than a few minutes at a time. When I did decide my back could stand a night off the ground, I stopped in at Charlie Slaughter's ranch.

Charlie was everything I was told he would be. His hair was grayer than a winter morning, and the lines on his face looked like a map of the Rocky Mountains. But from the way he moved, I doubted he was as old as he looked. He was chopping wood when I rode up, and making an easy job of it. His shirtsleeves were rolled up, and the muscles in his forearms looked like ropes.

I asked for a drink of water from the well. Charlie wiped sweat from his brow before answering. "He'p yourself," he said.

While drinking, I looked at his woodpile. It would take one man a week or more to split it all. "Looks like you plan on staying warm come winter," I said.

"If I don't wear myself out splitting it. But it's got to be done. Right now, though, I could use a cup of coffee. You're welcome to a cup."

We went inside, drank coffee, and talked a bit. Then Charlie stood up. "I'd best get back to the woodpile," he said. "If you don't mind waiting a spell, you're welcome to stay for supper."

"If you have a spare ax," I said, "I'd like to work for my

supper. Maybe together we can put a dent in that wood-pile?"

Charlie grinned. "Mister, you he'p me cut that woodpile down to size, and I'll feed you supper for a week."

We went to work splitting wood, and as men will do, soon we were having a friendly race. I was younger and stronger, but Charlie was better with an ax. It was neck and neck most of the evening, but Charlie came out a little ahead. The big loser was the woodpile.

Nothing builds a friendship faster than working shoulder to shoulder with a man, and by the time we quit swinging axes, each of us had a new respect for the other. The invitation to supper was extended to a bed for the night, and I accepted.

Through working together, and through talking over coffee and supper, I learned quite a bit about Charlie, all of it told in his own, slow, straightforward way.

Money was still tight, he said, so he did his own cooking, his own washing, and his own ranching. Come roundup and branding time, he would hire as many hands as he had to, and keep them on until the work was done. His ranch was just reaching the point where he could sell a few head every year . . . enough to pay the mortgage with a bit more to last until the next year.

Charlie had already made a drive this year, and he was disappointed with the results. "The market was down," he told me over supper. "Seemed like every rancher in the country was trying to sell cattle, and here I come with another herd.

"A month earlier and I'd have gotten twenty-five a head, but I had to haggle to get seventeen. I needed cash money, so I sold. It was enough to pay the mortgage, but come spring the banker'll be at me again. If it wasn't for my daughter I'd give this ranch to the bank, and tell 'em where to put it."

Charlie's cooking wasn't quite up to Snakepot's, but it

was a bunch better than mine, so I ate whatever he put in front of me. Later, sitting in front of the fireplace and drinking coffee, Charlie lit a pipe and told me about Alaska. He said much the same thing that Vance had, but Charlie had been to Alaska and brought it alive with his stories.

"She's a fearful land," he said. "Any man who goes into the interior and says he ain't afraid is either a liar or a fool. I've seen it so cold you couldn't sleep for the sound of trees splitting open. You can spit on a day like that, and it freezes before it hits the ground. A man gets caught in the open without food or shelter, or if he gets wet, he's dead.

"I've seen men go crazy in the summer from the mosquitoes, and run screaming into the brush, ripping at their clothes until they was buck naked. In the summer it's the mosquitoes and the bigness that drives a man crazy, and in the winter it's the cold and the loneliness.

"If that ain't enough, there's wolves big as a yearling cow, and bears that make a big grizzly look like a house pet. A man I know killed one that stood just over eleven feet.

"On top of that, there's plenty of Indians who'd love to put a bullet into a white man, and plenty of white men worse than a dozen Indians.

"Alaska is a wild, dangerous land, but I'll tell you something, there's no place on earth more beautiful, and no place I'd rather be, given the choice."

"If you liked it so much," I asked, "what made you leave?"

Charlie tapped the ashes from his pipe and took a drink of coffee. "Money," he said. "I plain ran out. It wouldn't have mattered much to me, but I have a daughter back East, and her husband had himself an accident. He's blind now, and it's been hard on them.

"So I came down here and started this ranch. I've made a bit of money, and most of it I send back to Marcella."

"What about driving cattle to Alaska? Do you think you'll ever get around to it?"

Charlie went to the stove and drained the coffeepot into his cup, then put on a fresh pot to boil. He came back and sat down, then refilled his pipe before answering.

"The truth is," he said, "I may never get it done. Oh, it makes sense. I still have friends in Alaska, and one of them writes me a letter now and again. Yes, sir, taking cattle to Alaska makes sense.

"They're finding gold all over the place, and people are swarming in from everywhere, and not one in a hundred can feed himself off the land. What's more, men grow up eating beef. They get a hankering for it.

"Getting a small herd in there will be hard, but it should be possible. And do you know what they're paying for beef? A dollar a pound on the hoof, that's what! If a man could get a hundred head in there he'd be set for life."

I whistled. "For that kind of money somebody will make the drive. Might as well be you."

He slowly shook his head. "I don't know. I'd sure like to try it, but if something happened to me, what would Marcella do? She's all the family I have, and her husband is a fine man. Without my help I don't know if they could make it."

It was well after dark when we both went to bed, and for a long time I stayed awake, thinking over what Charlie had told me about Alaska. A man could make a fortune driving cattle up there, but he'd have to be first. The moment somebody proved it could be done, everybody else would follow. I was sorry he wasn't going to try it.

Come morning, I was up early as ever, but even as my eyes opened I heard Charlie moving around in the kitchen and knew I'd found a man who was able to get up even earlier than I did. Rolling to a sitting position, I took a minute to get the grogginess out of my head, then put on my hat, pants, and boots in that order. Standing up, I belted on my Colt, stretched, and went into the kitchen.

Charlie was hard at work on breakfast, but I went on past him and outside. I washed my face and took care of my morning chores, then rolled a smoke and went back inside. We ate breakfast, and I helped him with the few dishes. For a time we sat and talked, but daylight was burning and about nine o'clock I saddled Apache and rode southwest, a bit of fresh food behind my saddle.

Most of my time had been spent learning all I could about Vance Douglas's ranch and the cattle on it. It was a fine ranch, and no two ways about it. There was water and grass in plenty, several places where a man could drive cattle to keep them out of the wind and the snow, and the cattle themselves were thick as ants at a picnic.

There were, I knew, ranches down in Texas, and even a couple in Wyoming and Montana, that would make the Douglas ranch look small. But nowhere had I seen one better run than the ranch I was riding across. Barring bad luck, it was also going to be a big money-maker, and a cowboy's dream to work on.

When I finally rode back to Vance's ranch house I knew his land almost as well as he did, and I knew more about the condition of his herd.

Angie was working in a small flower garden near the house when I rode in. She was wearing a simple green dress and her hair was pulled back in a ponytail, but she was still the prettiest thing I'd seen in four days of looking at some of the most beautiful country on earth.

She smiled and waved as I rode in, and I returned both. Then I went to see Vance. We had some talking to do about his herd.

Vance was sitting in a chair on the front porch, reading the Bible and drinking lemonade. Me, I was dirty and bearded from all those days on the trail, but I wanted to talk to Vance while everything was still fresh in my mind. I tied Apache to a rail of the corral until I could care for him properly and walked over to the porch.

When Vance saw me, he marked his spot in the Bible and carefully laid it on the banister. "I asked you to look at my ranch," he said, "not wear it back here."

"I guess I did bring back a few pounds," I said. "It'll take a river to wash it all off."

"Well, what do you think of the place?"

"It's a fine spread," I said. "But your cattle are another story. They need some attention."

"Huh, what kind of attention? Ted and Jules have been all over the range this summer, and they tell me the herd is doing well. Multiplying like rabbits, is how Jules put it to me."

"Yes, sir," I said, "and that's just the problem. The herd is growing too fast. Were you planning to make another drive this fall?"

"Hadn't thought about it, but we usually cull a hundred head or so."

"If you want to keep your herd healthy you'll have to drive at least four times that number, maybe more."

"What? I don't have more than a thousand head. Cutting four hundred head won't leave much in the way of breeding stock for next year."

"Ted and Jules are both good men, but I've spent most of my time in Texas, and down there you learn how to find cattle in some of the most god-awful brush you've ever seen. You don't have a thousand head of cattle, you have at least fifteen hundred head, and maybe more. You have way too many old bulls, and quite a few cows that won't last the winter. Your herd needs to be culled in the worst way."

"Can't it wait until spring? I made one drive earlier this summer, and the market is down."

Generally, I smoke in the morning, or late at night, and

sometimes when I'm tired and hungry. But most often I smoke when I'm trying to think. So I rolled a smoke and lit it. "It can wait until spring," I said, "but I'd recommend against it. Your range isn't overstocked, but you have at least five or six hundred head of cattle that aren't doing you a bit of good. Mostly, you need to get rid of them to make sure the others last the winter. Six hundred extra mouths might not ruin your range, but they sure won't do it any good. You have grass and water enough for two thousand head or more, but only if they're spread out and pushed from one place to another. But the main thing is this, if you wait until spring, a lot of those cattle won't be alive. Drive 'em in now and you'll make some money. Wait until spring and all they'll be is coyote food."

Vance Douglas stood up and looked out over his land, hands in his back pockets. "Let's go in and get a cup of coffee," he said. "It looks like we have some work to do."

We walked into the house and sat down. For better than an hour we talked about the best way to get all the culls gathered without hiring half the cowboys in Wyoming to hunt for them. At last we had all the details worked out; then the real work started.

CHAPTER 4

FOR THE NEXT month we worked like dogs. Vance hired two extra men, but even with them pitching in, we worked harder than I've ever worked in my life. Yet in the end we had every extra bull, every too-old or sickly cow, gathered into a herd that we pushed down to Cheyenne. Vance sold seven hundred and twenty-three head of mixed cattle for just over fourteen dollars a head. Every dollar of it was money to the good, and Vance realized it.

"Brent," he said, "I never thought I'd be happy to sell cattle at these prices, but I am. I still can't believe I had that many useless cattle on my range."

"It happens," I said. "The herd should be in good shape for several years to come, with just a little care at roundup."

"That's true, and it's you I have to thank for it. I've never hired a foreman, but it sure looks like I need one. I'd like you to take the job."

"Me? Ted and Jules have both been on the ranch a lot longer than I have."

"Yes, but I don't think either of them would mind having you as foreman. They simply don't have your experience. No, I want you to take the job. I'll double your salary and give you complete charge of the herd. You'll hire and fire, and generally oversee everything."

"What will you do?"

He smiled. "I'll oversee you."

I returned his smile. "In that case, I'll take the job, with thanks."

"No thanks are necessary. You earned it."

Over the next month I became comfortable with the role of foreman, and found I liked it. And if I was ever fortunate enough to own a ranch of my own, the experience would be invaluable.

Somehow over that month I began spending more time with Angie. I don't know exactly how it happened, but suddenly we were taking long walks together, and soon we were holding hands. Without planning it, I fell in love with her, and that was a damn fool thing to let happen.

It was bad enough that Angie was the boss's daughter, and I was only a working cowboy, even if I had been promoted to foreman. But I hadn't forgotten about Fergus Thornton and the reward he still had on my head.

The smart thing would have been to ride away and not look back. It also would have been the right thing to do and, I suppose, the courageous thing. But I couldn't do it. I told myself that Fergus Thornton was behind me, that my new name meant he'd lost my trail for good.

Deep down inside I didn't believe a word of it, but for once in my life I listened to my heart instead of my head. It was the biggest mistake I ever made.

It was late in October, with the full moon above us and the chill of winter already in the air, when I kissed Angie for the first time. And knowing I was being seven kinds of a fool, I asked her to marry me.

Her arms were on my shoulders, her hands locked behind my neck, and even in the moonlight I could see the blue of her eyes. "Yes," she said. "Yes, I'll marry you. I love you, Brent Griffin. I have since the day you knocked me down back in Slater."

Never in my life had I felt anything like what I felt for Angie, but when she called me Brent Griffin a chill went through me. I wasn't brave enough or strong enough to walk away from her as I should have done, yet I knew that she had to be told the truth. I had to tell Angie who I was, and what I was running from. What I didn't know was how.

The next morning I walked from the bunkhouse to the main house, and a longer walk I never took. My heart was beating heavy and felt like a chunk of lead in my chest. When Vance answered the door there was a big smile on his face that I couldn't match.

"Come in, Brent, come in," he said. "Angie told me the good news, so I know why you're here. Come on in. We have things to talk about."

I went inside, and Angie was there, sitting on a sofa and looking lovely. When I came into the room she stood up and came to me, taking my hands in hers. "You look like you've been run over by a stampede of wild horses," she said. "Why the gloomy face? Having second thoughts?"

"No," I said. "I love you, Angie. There's nothing in this world I want more than to marry you and to spend the rest of my life with you. I'm not having second thoughts, but after you hear what I have to say, you may think twice about marrying me."

The happy look left her face. "Why, Brent? What's wrong?"

Taking a deep breath, I started talking before I lost my nerve. "There's something I have to tell both of you," I said. "My name isn't Brent Griffin. My real name is Clay Kerrigan."

Angie's lips were parted and I couldn't read her eyes.

Vance's voice was hard, tight, and serious. "You'd best tell us about it," he said. "Let's go into the kitchen and get a cup of coffee."

We went into the kitchen, and over coffee I laid out the whole story. When I finished, Angie let out a deep breath. "Thank God," she said. "I imagined all kinds of things when you told me your name wasn't Brent Griffin. I thought you must be a bank robber, or something even worse. But you haven't done anything wrong, Brent . . . or Clay. This is going to take some getting used to."

"It's Brent," I said. "I have to use that name. Maybe I'll always have to use it."

"It doesn't matter what I call you," Angie said. "You haven't done anything wrong. It wasn't your fault."

"That's how I see it, too," Vance said. "But you have to understand: Angie is my only daughter, and I don't want her hurt. Do you think you've lost this Thornton fellow for good?"

"I honestly don't know, Vance. This is a big, big country, but it's still short on people and towns. There's always the chance some traveler will recognize me and carry word to Fergus Thornton.

"I love Angie," I said. "I love her with all my heart, and I wouldn't knowingly put her in danger. I'll fully understand if you ask me to ride away and not come back. But I hope you won't do that."

Vance ran his fingers through his hair and said, "Angie is all in this world that means a thing to me. I won't lie, Brent. I have my doubts. This whole affair worries me. But I know Angie, and she would never forgive me if I sent you away. Besides, she was right in saying you've done nothing wrong. Thornton is the one in the wrong here, and there should be a law against what he's done."

"Thornton is a Texas rancher," I said. "One of the biggest. In Texas, ranchers still write their own laws."

"Maybe, but things are changing, Brent. There should be a way of making Fergus Thornton call off the bounty he's put on your head."

"Fergus isn't a bad man," I said. "Not in the usual sense of the word. He's a hard man who's lived a hard life, and he believes justice is something you handle yourself. Law and order may be coming, but it isn't here yet. Not even in the cities, let alone out on the range. I know Fergus, and he won't stop looking for me until one of us is dead. I'm sorry, but that's how it is."

"Then let's hope he never finds you," Vance said. "Now, we have a wedding to plan, and I don't know the first thing about it. But I'll wager the ranch that Angie has a few ideas on the subject."

"You know I have," Angie said. "All I need to know is when. We haven't even talked about a date."

The thought of a date had never entered my mind, so we talked about it. After some thought we all agreed on the second Sunday in April. That was almost six months away, and seemed an appropriate length of time to be engaged. It also seemed like an eternity.

Vance wanted me to move into the main house, but I wouldn't have felt comfortable there and said as much. So I stayed in the bunkhouse, and I courted Angie, counting down the days until we were married.

November came in cold, but without snow. December made up for it. The snow came early and fast. Blizzard followed blizzard, and cattle started dying from the cold and from lack of food.

By the end of December the entire territory was buried under several feet of snow, and in places the drifts piled twice as high as a man's head. The moment we realized how bad things were we started scouring the range, trying to gather all of Vance's cattle into one herd.

A long rise of land about three miles north of the ranch house offered the perfect windbreak, and we pushed every cow we could find right up to it. Even out of the wind, the snow was so deep the horses had trouble making headway, but the cattle soon packed the snow down along the rise, and we started hauling hay.

Only the fact that Vance had planted, cut, and cured so much hay, and the fact that we had culled the herd, saved most of his cattle. Other ranchers weren't so lucky. By the middle of January it was plain that half the ranchers in the area were out of business and most of the others would be years recovering. And spring was still two months away.

With Vance's herd safely tucked in along the rise and well fed with hay, the chance finally came to get away for a few days. Most of the big ranchers had all the men they needed, but a few ranchers were short, and Charlie Slaughter was one of these. We got word that he hadn't been able to find anyone willing or able to herd cattle in that weather for what he could afford to pay.

The temperature had bottomed out and it was brutally cold. People stayed inside as much as possible, and a lot of cattle were left to die. It was something like thirty below, and staying indoors was the smart move, but Charlie Slaughter needed help.

Charlie wasn't in the cattle business for personal gain. He was trying to build a ranch for the sole purpose of giving his daughter and her family an easier life. If he lost the ranch he wouldn't be able to do that.

Knowing it was a foolish thing to do, I climbed out of my bunk on a frigid morning near the end of January, put on two extra shirts and an extra pair of wool pants, and decided to see if I could help Charlie. Vance had bought all of us sheepskin coats the moment the weather turned cold, and that went over everything else. Belting on my Colt and slapping my Stetson on my head, I went over to the main house and told Vance where I was going.

"That's a long, cold ride you're planning," he said. "The wind's picking up again and it looks like more snow. You ride careful. Weather like this can kill a man fast."

I nodded. "I've ridden cold country before," I said. "I know enough to be afraid."

Angie came into the kitchen then, still looking half asleep, but beautiful in spite of it. She wasn't happy when I told her where I was going, but she understood. "I like Charlie," she said. "I'd hate to see him lose his ranch."

I went over to see Snakepot for food to take along and

found myself forced to eat a hot breakfast. "Only a fool goes out in weather like this with an empty belly," he grumbled. "You eat all you can hold and maybe you'll reach Charlie's ranch alive."

I ate all I could, then went out and saddled Apache. A bigger horse might have been better, but I knew Apache and trusted him to get me there and back alive. We left the stable and rode north into a bitter wind that hit us right in the face.

I'd grown a beard to help ward off the cold, but against that wind it was useless. Pulling my hat low and scrunching deep into the warmth of the fleece-lined collar on my coat, I pointed Apache into the teeth of the wind.

Apache didn't like the wind or the cold any more than I did, but he lowered his head and walked into it, willing to go where I wished. The truth is, I didn't worry much about Apache. He was from wild mustang stock, and his winter coat of hair was thick and nearly impervious to the cold. If I helped him find browse and didn't push too hard, he'd be fine.

The trick to riding in weather like that is to go slow, stop frequently, and take care of frostbite before it does damage. But maybe the most important thing of all is to avoid working up a sweat. Sweat makes the inner layers of clothing damp, and it puts a thin sheet of moisture next to the skin. When you stop moving that thin sheet of moisture freezes and you die.

We stopped every couple of hours, and each time I built a small fire out of the wind and made coffee. While it boiled, I scraped away snow so Apache could get at the grass beneath it. That evening I was lucky enough to find a draw that offered shelter from the wind, and there we made camp.

I can't say I was comfortable at any time during the trip, but on the other hand, it wasn't as bad as it might seem to someone who's never spent time in the cold.

When we finally reached Charlie's cabin it was empty. There was a note on the table saying he was out gathering cattle, and that anyone who happened along should make himself at home, so that's what I did.

First I put Apache inside Charlie's stable, rubbed him down, and gave him hay and oats. Then I went into the house and stoked the fire. The ashes in the fireplace still had life, but not much. That meant Charlie had likely been out several hours. At his age, and in that weather, I was sure he'd be in soon, but he was a stubborn old cuss and might try pushing his luck beyond what common sense told him was safe.

The day wore on and still there was no sign of Charlie.

As night grew close I was worried enough to go looking for him, but as I reached for my coat the door opened and Charlie stumbled in amid a shower of snow.

His breath had covered his eyebrows and mustache with frost, and he was shaking uncontrollably, but several cups of coffee in front of the fireplace helped him recover. Only after half an hour had passed was he able to talk.

"I was so anxious to get my bones warm that I never gave a second thought to you being here," he said. "What on earth brings you over here in weather like this?"

"We were lucky with Vance's herd," I said. "He lost a few cattle, but not enough to matter. I wasn't so sure about your herd. How are they doing?"

Charlie shook his head. "What herd? My cattle are all but wiped out. I cut a little hay and kept a good-sized field from the cattle all summer. Figured to drive them in there when the first snow came. But I sure never counted on a winter like this."

"Nobody figured on it. Have you saved any cattle at all?"

"Maybe seventy-five head. Half my cattle are dead already, and the other half are going fast."

"Maybe together we can save enough of them to get you through next year."

"I plan on saving all I can," Charlie said, "but it won't be enough. Come spring this whole territory is going to be covered with dead cattle. Never saw anything like it."

"In the morning we'll take stock," I said. "I can stay a few days, maybe a week."

"I appreciate it," Charlie said. "Not many would have made the ride you did just to help an old man he barely knows."

We turned in early, and even through the solid walls of the cabin I could hear the howl of the north wind.

It was still howling when we crawled out of bed the next morning. We ate breakfast in silence, listening to the continuing fury of the winter storm. When the food was gone, I drained my coffee cup and looked at Charlie. "A man could freeze to death in weather like this," I said.

"That's a fact. Only a damn fool would go out chasing cows on a day like this."

For a time we sat silent again. At last I stood up. "To hell with the weather," I said. "Let's go save some cows."

Charlie grinned. "Why not? I always was a damn fool, and I'm too old to change now."

Mister, if you think we had anything like fun, you've never straddled a horse in below-zero weather and rode into the teeth of a blowing snowstorm for hours on end. We stopped three times throughout the day to build a fire and eat a little hot food, but when we stomped back into the cabin that night I felt like an icicle.

I ended up staying with Charlie for almost two weeks, and most of that time was spent in the saddle. He was right about the condition of his herd. Something like half were already dead, and a lot of the rest were too far gone to save. So we concentrated on heifers and young bulls, hoping to save enough breeding stock to let Charlie get through another year.

All things considered, we did well, but not nearly well enough. When at last we'd done all there was to do, we had just over two hundred head of cattle in a position where they stood a good chance of lasting the winter.

Many a man has built a ranch with fewer cattle than we saved, and had Charlie owned his land free and clear, and if he could have afforded to go three or four years without showing a profit, things might have been different. But his land was mortgaged to the hilt, and he had his daughter to think about. The coming year didn't look promising for Charlie Slaughter.

By the time I rode back to the Douglas ranch I was done in. When I walked into the bunkhouse Jules asked how things had gone, but I didn't say a word. I dropped onto my bunk without taking off my clothes and slept for twelve straight hours.

CHAPTER 5

AS IF TRYING to make up for the hard winter, spring came early to the land. March came in more like June, and the snow melted and vanished in a few days' time. What it revealed was ugly. Thousands of bloating carcasses littered the range, and only a few fortunate ranchers had enough cattle to keep going.

To their credit, the banks worked with the ranchers as much as possible, and if there was a way to extend a mortgage or hand out another loan, the banks usually found it. But some ranchers were simply too far in debt and had too few cattle remaining. Charlie was one of them.

He came by the ranch toward the middle of March, and he looked good, considering what the winter had done to him. Charlie ate his supper with us at the main house, and Angie told him how sorry she was about the cattle he'd lost.

"It's a tough row to hoe," he said, "but don't count me out yet. The note on my ranch isn't due for several months yet, and I've a few ideas on how to meet it."

Angie and Vance both nodded as he said this, and no doubt they thought Charlie was trying to put the best face on things to stop them from feeling sorry for him. But there was a twinkle in his eye and a sincerity to his voice that made me believe he really did have an idea or two.

When Charlie was ready to leave, I walked out to the stable with him. "Griffin," he said, "I'm still in your debt. I'm mighty beholding to you, and I don't know how to repay what you did for me."

"There's nothing to repay," I said. "What I did was only one neighbor helping another. I'm sorry we couldn't save more than we did."

Charlie laughed. "It might be we saved enough," he said. "Yes, sir, it might be we saved just enough."

Realization dawned on me. "Charlie, you old coot, you're going to do it, aren't you. You're going to take those cattle to Alaska."

"I sure am. Leastways, I'm going to try. It'll take a month or so to pull things together. I have to line up a train, and I'm waiting for word on the steamships, but we'll pull out sometime next month.

"I also need to hire two or three good men. Don't suppose you'd like to be one of them?"

I shook my head. "Charlie, I got to admit, it sounds like the trip of a lifetime, but I'm getting hitched next month, and *that's* a trip I've been wanting to take for a long, long time."

"I don't blame you," he said. "Miss Angie is sure enough a fine-looking woman and sweet as maple sugar. Looks like your summer is going to be a darn sight better than mine."

"Charlie, I never wanted anything in my life more than I want Angie. When I'm with her I feel like I'm walking six inches off the ground. But do you know what? Every time I think about the wedding my hands get sweaty, my mouth goes dry, and I feel like there's a buffalo dancing in my stomach."

Charlie already had his pipe going, and he blew out a cloud of smoke. "Griffin, truth be told, I think every man feels like that, if they'd admit it. My Colleen was the most wonderful woman who ever lived. She had red hair, green eyes, and a temper worse than a bear with a sore tooth. But, Lordy, how I loved that woman. She meant more than my life. But I felt exactly like you do when marrying time came around. Facing that preacher with her scared me worse than facing down a whole tribe of wild Indians."

"That puts it down just about right," I said. "Does it get easier after the wedding?"

"Son, after the wedding you'll be so busy loving that woman you won't remember anything else."

A picture of Angie came into my mind. "Yes, sir," I said. "I can see how that might be the case."

Charlie climbed onto his horse with an ease that gave lie to the wrinkles on his face. He rode out, raising his pipe in farewell. I walked back to the house, feeling a good deal less nervous than before.

April came, and with it, the land turned green and lovely. On the third day of April, with a warm, gentle breeze blowing in from the south, with the birds singing and the sun shining, I drove Angie into town. It was really a trip to buy supplies for the ranch, so I hitched a team to the biggest wagon we had, and with Angie sitting beside me, we went down the road to Slater.

There may be better things in life than sitting beside the woman you love, listening to the birds sing, and feeling the warmth of the spring on your face . . . but if so, I've never found them.

Letting Angie off at the dress shop, I drove on down to the mercantile and went inside. The ranch was low on everything after the long, hard winter, and it took some time to get all I wanted in a stack. Then it all had to be loaded into the wagon. Mr. Cromberg was working alone in the store, and he's a small man with a bad back, so I did all the loading myself.

Most of the things I bought were heavy or awkward to handle, and the heavy Colt around my waist was in the way. I removed the gun belt and hung it on a hitch rail where it would be out of the way, yet close at hand if needed.

With that done, I rolled up my sleeves and went to

loading the wagon. It didn't take long to break a sweat. With the wagon nearly loaded, I stopped to wipe my brow and saw Angie walking down the boardwalk toward me. There was a bounce in her step and a smile on her face that made men turn their heads to watch her pass. She didn't seem to notice.

Angie was almost to me when the smile suddenly left her face. Her eyes were looking past me, and they were filled with terror. I started to turn and look behind me, but Angie lunged at me, knocking me back several steps as a pistol roared only a few yards away.

My head turned toward the sound and I saw him, a big man with long black hair and a Colt extended in his right hand. Instinctively I grabbed for my own pistol, remembering too late it was hanging on the hitch rail, and Angie had pushed me even further from it.

Grabbing wildly at the wagon, my hand closed painfully around a spool of barbed wire. Ignoring the pain, I threw it at the man with all my strength. He tried to sidestep, but the heavy spool of wire caught him on the shoulder, knocking him off balance. His Colt fired, the bullet sailing harmlessly into the air.

I grabbed a pitchfork from the wagon and charged the man. He caught his balance, but then I was on him. Just as his Colt fired I slammed upward with the pitchfork, and the long tines buried themselves under the man's breastbone and angled upward. The shock ran through my hands and up to my shoulders.

He dropped the Colt and grabbed the pitchfork handle, a look of horror on his face. He screamed and went to his knees, and for a minute he stayed like that, trying to pull the pitchfork free. Then he fell sideways into the mud. He died there, still holding the handle of the pitchfork.

I turned back to Angie, and my heart seemed to stop in my chest. She was lying in the street, her eyes closed and her dress stained with blood. I ran to her and scooped her into my arms. I looked about wildly at the people rushing to see what the shooting was all about.

Angie made a groaning sound and it was only then I realized she was still alive. That snapped me out of the shock I'd been experiencing. If Angie was still breathing, there was a chance she wasn't hurt too seriously. Looking around, I screamed for someone to get a doctor. As it happened, the doctor was already on his way, shoving through the still gathering crowd.

He took one look at Angie and led the way to his office. The next half hour was a nightmare, but at last the doctor came out of the small room where I'd carried Angie. He was wiping his hands on a towel, and until he spoke it was as if the whole world hung in the balance.

"She'll be fine," he said. "The bullet cut across the top of her shoulder and did very little damage. The shock made her pass out. She'll be sore for a while, but in a couple of weeks she'll be good as new."

"Can I see her?"

"I don't see why not, but only for a minute. I gave her something to ease the pain, and it's going to make her a little woozy, I'm afraid. But you'd better let me take a look at you first. I doubt if it's serious, but it has to hurt."

"What has to hurt?"

"Are you daft? Your side, of course. You've been shot, man!"

It was only then I realized my left side was hurting. Looking down, I found a wide streak of blood. I'd been so intent on whether Angie was going to live or die that I hadn't noticed my own wound.

The doctor—his name was Peter Tomsier—cleaned the shallow groove cut by the bullet, dabbed it with something that burned like hellfire, and finished the job with a bandage. Then I went in to see Angie.

Her eyes were closed, and for a moment I thought she was sleeping. But as I moved closer her eyes opened about halfway and she smiled. I took her hand in mine. It was tiny, soft, warm. "I'm sorry, Angie. I'm so very sorry."

She wet her lips with her tongue. The need for sleep was evident in her voice. "I'm so . . . glad you're all right. . . . Darling . . . I love you."

Angie closed her eyes again, her breathing turned regular, and I knew she was sleeping. Still holding her hand, I looked down at her. "I love you, Angie. I love you too much to see you hurt because of me."

I drove the supply wagon back out to the ranch. Telling Vance what happened wasn't an easy thing to do. He's a strong man, but the news about Angie shook him all the way through. The color drained from his face, and his hands began to shake so badly that coffee sloshed from the cup he was holding and splattered on the floor.

He quickly saddled a horse and left for Slater at a gallop. I saddled Apache and followed him into town, but not before taking the time to pack my gear. I took my time getting to town and did a lot of thinking along the way. The thoughts weren't pleasant.

It was almost as though I'd been in a dream, and only on the ride out to the ranch did I awaken. Angie had almost been killed. It was only by the grace of God that she was still alive.

Anger was growing inside me. Anger at myself for putting Angie in a position where she could be hit by a bullet, and anger at Fergus Thornton for the hatred that caused him to put the price on my head.

It was time to finish it. It was time to end the feud one way or another. I was going to say good-bye to Angie, and then I intended to ride back to Texas and have things out with Fergus Thornton.

The truth is, although Fergus was a pigheaded, self-righteous, arrogant man, there was much about him I found to admire. When Fergus came to Texas all those years ago it was a much wilder place than now. To build his ranch Fergus fought Indians, wild animals, nature, and white men worse than all the rest combined.

In all his fights he came out on top, and in doing so he built something few men could equal and any man would be proud to call his own.

But because of Fergus, Angie was almost killed. The anger aroused by that thought was a white-hot fire burning in my chest.

The feud had to end. Fergus Thornton had to be stopped, and if that meant one of us had to die, well, so be it.

I rode into Slater almost two hours behind Vance. When I went to see Angie he met me outside. "She's my only daughter, Brent. Do you know what that means?"

"I know, Vance. I know. I came to say good-bye."

Vance lowered his eyes. "It will break her heart."

"It'll save her life."

"Brent, it isn't that I want you to go, either. But I have to put Angie first."

My voice didn't sound quite right. "I feel the same way, Vance. I won't risk putting her in danger again."

The moment I walked in to see her, Angie seemed to read my thoughts. Taking her hand, I sat down in a chair next to the bed.

"Angie, I love you."

"And I love you, Brent."

"Unh-uh. From now on my name is Clay Kerrigan."

"I don't care what your name is. But promise me you won't leave."

"I—I have to, Angie. It's the only way."

"But we love each other. We can make it through this if we do it together."

"No, Angie, we can't. I'm sorry, Angie. Sorrier than you'll ever know. But it has to be this way. Fergus knows where I am now, and he'll send someone else. If I stayed, someone else would come along to collect the reward.

Maybe several men would come. We were lucky this time, Angie. Next time you might be killed."

"I don't care. If you leave, I might as well be dead."

Tears were running down her cheeks, and I couldn't think of anything to say that wouldn't make her hurt even worse, so I said nothing. She squeezed my hand. "Where will you go?"

"Texas. Angie, if I don't stop him, no one will. I can't run and hide all my life."

"You told me yourself you couldn't get close to him. He has too many men. Clay, I've never asked you to do anything you didn't believe was right, but I'm asking you not to go back there. Promise me, Clay. If you really love me, promise you won't go back to Texas."

There was nothing else I could do. "I promise, Angie. I won't go after Thornton. But I still have to leave."

"Leave if you have to, but I'm not giving up on you. Somehow, some way, we'll be together again. I swear it."

I nodded. "I pray you're right." Leaning over, I kissed her gently on the lips. "Good-bye, Angie."

I walked out of the room without looking back. Behind me I could hear Angie crying softly. At that moment it felt like Fergus Thornton had already won.

Vance was waiting for me outside. He handed me a thick envelope. "You have some wages coming," he said. "I— well, I added a little to see you through."

"You didn't have to do that, Vance."

"I wanted to. Look, Brent, I don't know how to say this, but I'll try. I feel like I'm running you off, and that's not how I mean it. If there's ever a way you can return without putting Angie in danger, you'll be welcome. I don't hold anything against you."

"Thanks, Vance. That means a lot."

I rode out of Slater and headed northwest. I had no idea where I was going, and it didn't seem to matter. It was only when I made camp for the night that I counted the money inside the envelope Vance handed me. I'd had two months' pay coming, and that was a total of one hundred and sixty dollars.

The envelope held my one-sixty, plus five hundred extra. All I could do was shake my head.

CHAPTER 6

APACHE AND I hunted out the wildest, most desolate stretch of the Laramie Mountains we could find, and for ten days I did nothing more than ride by day, camp by night, and feel sorry for myself. On the eleventh day it rained, and the best shelter I could find wasn't enough to keep me dry.

I huddled under an outcropping of rock that kept the direct rain off, but enough blew in from the front to make me miserable. I sat there, getting wetter and wetter, until I was soaked through to the bone. There wasn't a stick of dry wood to be found nearby, and that meant no fire and no hot food or coffee.

For a long time I sat there. Angie was strong on my mind, and somehow the rain made every problem I had seem a thousand times worse. In short, you never saw a sorrier sight than I was right then.

In one sense, though, sitting there in the rain was good for me. It finally came to me just how sorry I was acting, and how much Angie was depending on me to find a way out of my troubles. She was hurting as much as I was, but I'd been so busy feeling sorry for myself that I didn't think of her feelings. It made me ashamed.

So I sat there a while longer and did some serious thinking. If I couldn't ride to Texas and have it out with Fergus, then it seemed I had little choice but to find a place where I could live a reasonably normal life outside of even his long reach.

It might be that Angie and I could never be together

again. It was a horrible thought, but I was realistic enough to know it was more than possible.

The thought that suddenly popped into my mind was in many ways an obvious one, but I'd been so filled with thoughts of Angie that it hadn't registered. Alaska! Charlie Slaughter was about to start a trip to Alaska that would make history if he succeeded. He'd already asked me to ride along, so why not go? I couldn't think of a way to put more distance between Fergus and myself than by going to Alaska.

Charlie had described Alaska as a wild, savage land, but there were towns in Alaska and even the beginnings of cities. It was a tremendous gamble, but why not take it? There was nothing to lose, and everything to gain.

I'd unsaddled Apache so he could browse and rest while I waited out the rain. Not wanting him to wander too far away, I'd hobbled him with a length of rope that joined his front legs together. He could walk like that, but he couldn't run or even trot. It was still raining, but I was already wet, so I went looking for him. At first he wasn't to be found, but when I gave out a loud whistle, he answered with a whinny.

Working toward the sound, I finally found Apache. He'd found a spot where one heck of a wind had blown down a few hundred trees and left them in a tangled mess. Where Apache stood, the fallen trees had formed a jumble of pine boughs with an opening beneath large enough for a horse to walk in. While I was sitting back there getting soaked and hungry, Apache was dry and had a belly full of grass.

"Sometimes," I said, "I wonder which of us is smarter."

Apache cocked his head and gave me a look that said he knew darn well which . . . and he was probably right.

I led him back to where I'd left his saddle, and we took off for Charlie Slaughter's ranch in the rain. Apache bucked three or four times before letting me have control, but his heart wasn't in it. With the rain beating down on both of us, I started the ride back to see Charlie.

What worried me most about my plan was reaching Charlie's ranch without being seen. There were a couple of ranches between his place and that of Vance Douglas, but their houses were less than twelve miles apart. That would put me terribly close to Angie, and neighbors have a way of spreading word about anything and everything.

It wasn't that I didn't want to see Angie. I wanted to see her so much it hurt. But to see her again would only increase the pain for both of us. Assuming Charlie hadn't left already, he would certainly be going soon, so I shouldn't be around more than a few days at most. And I could trust Charlie not to tell anyone I was around.

When I rode up to Charlie's cabin he was gone, but an hour later he came riding in wearing a suit, and I knew it for the one he usually wore to church. That had to mean it was Sunday.

His wrinkled old face broke into a smile when he stepped through the door and saw me sitting there.

"Come in and make yourself at home," I said. "There's coffee on."

"That's real neighborly of you," he said mockingly. "Don't suppose you'd have a bite of lunch to go along with it."

"There's food," I said. "But you'll have to cook it yourself if you want it to be eatable. Do a good job and I might even hire you on as cook. A man gets real tired of eating his own cooking."

"I'll bet you can cook as well as anyone," he said. "You only claim you can't so someone else will do it."

"If you think that," I said, "I will cook lunch. But you have to eat it."

"Nope, you just made a believer out of me. Reckon I'll do the cooking, after all."

He laughed and held out his hand. I shook it. His grip

was like iron. "It's good to see you, boy," he said. "I figured you were long gone."

"So did I. Guess you heard what happened?"

"Sure. It's been the main topic of gossip since you rode away."

"Guess you know what brought me back, too?"

"I'm hoping I do. You want to go along on the drive to Alaska. Can't think of any other reason why you'd be here."

"That's it. If you're still going, and if you still want me along."

"I'm going. There's no choice if I want to keep out of the poorhouse. As for wanting you along, there's not a man I'd rather have."

"I might draw trouble."

"Boy, me and trouble been saddle partners off and on since I was fourteen. Now, what name do you want me to call you?"

"Clay Kerrigan. Whatever happens, that's my name from now on."

"All right, Clay. You can come along, and welcome. I've hired two men, and we're all set to go, but we have to wait until the right train comes along. If all goes right, we'll start the cattle toward the railroad next Friday, and put them on the train Monday morning. Once that's done, we won't have much to keep us busy until we reach the coast."

"It sounds good," I said. "But if it's all right with you, I'd like to lay low until we leave. If Angie learns I'm here she'll . . . well, I'd rather she didn't know."

"You might not have to worry about that, Clay. Angie has been gone most of a week."

"Gone? What do you mean, gone? She should still be in bed with that shoulder."

"That's what I said to Vance this morning. He said she was in Cheyenne, but didn't say why."

"Did he say when she would be back?"

"Nope. Just said she was too stubborn to stay in bed, and that she was in Cheyenne."

"Well, maybe it's for the best . . ."

Charlie went to get out of his suit, and I poured another cup of coffee. Why should I be so upset that Angie was gone? Was I fool enough to think she would shut herself in a room and spend the rest of her life pining for me? No, Angie needed to live. She needed to get away, to meet new people, to forget all about me.

Women love as strongly and as passionately as any man, and maybe more so. But while I'm no expert on the subject, it's been my experience that women also have a practical outlook on love that most men seem to lack. Women cry and hurt and mourn when a love is lost, but when the crying and the hurting and the mourning end, they pick up the pieces of their lives and move on. They look at the smooth stretch of road ahead rather than the bumpy stretch of road they've just crossed.

I wished with all my heart that I was capable of doing exactly that, but I knew it wasn't to be. Wherever I went, whatever the road ahead held in store, Angie would be right there in my heart.

When Charlie came back into the kitchen he was wearing range clothes, and looked more like the man I'd chased cattle through a blizzard with. He fixed lunch and we ate, then Charlie stoked up his pipe while I rolled a smoke.

"If you're looking to keep low, and want to stay busy at the same time, how would you like to sell some cattle for me?"

"Be glad to. Just point where you want them taken."

"It won't be a major job, but some of the cattle have to go. We're taking the best of the lot with us . . . exactly one hundred and twelve head. That leaves about a hundred and forty that we can't take."

"Why not?"

"Practical reasons, mostly. We can handle any number of cattle on the railroad, but steamships are another matter. We'll likely have to split the herd onto a couple of ships as it is.

"And when we do reach Alaska, we'll wish we'd left even more cattle behind. It'll take a ton of work and a lot of luck to get even a hundred head through those mountain passes. Any more would be pushing it. Besides, I need money to make this drive, and selling those extra cattle should give me enough to get through. So I found a man over near Laramie who's willing to pay top dollar for breeding stock.

"The boys I hired are coming in tomorrow, and I was going to help push the cattle over to his ranch. But it might be better if you go instead. It won't take more than three or four days round-trip, but that'll give me time to put a few finishing touches on my plans."

"It beats sitting around here doing nothing," I said. "Just tell me how to find the man with the money, and I'll take him a herd of cattle."

We spent most of the evening talking about the trip to Alaska. The next morning we were out of bed by five-thirty, and an hour later the two men Charlie hired for the drive came riding up to the door. I got to know them over breakfast, and as expected, Charlie showed he knew how to pick men.

Paul Donica was twenty-three or so, and a little shy of six feet. His hair was blond, and he had a quick sense of humor. His hands were work-hardened, and everything about him spoke of competence.

Billy Curtis was almost four years younger, but a little taller. He had a ready laugh, but when he spoke of cattle there was a no-nonsense attitude about him that made me think he'd had more experience than his age would suggest.

Both of them showed a willingness to work; they were the kind of men you'd pick to ride the river with.

After breakfast I went out and saddled Apache, then we rode out to the herd. Billy had been over to separate the herd a couple of days earlier, and he knew them by heart. He cut a she cow from the rest and started her down the trail. The other cattle lined up behind her and followed along as pretty as you please.

Every herd has an animal somewhere in it that the others will naturally follow. I've known ranchers who used the same lead cow on a half dozen drives, refusing to sell it at market, being willing to walk it all the way back home instead.

Our drive was a short one, and we reached the rancher near Fort Laramie just over forty-eight hours after Billy started that first cow up the trail. Dewey Wheeler was short and round, and had a big mustache and a voice like a frog. But he knew cattle. He took one look at the bunch we brought in and offered twenty-five dollars a head right on the spot. I said yes, and he paid in cash.

With no cattle to slow us down on the way back, we made a quick ride of it. But when we rode up to the cabin there was a buggy sitting in front. Thinking nothing of it, I opened the door and stepped inside. Charlie was sitting at the table, and right across from him sat Angie. She looked up at me and her blue eyes seemed to glow. "Hello, Clay," she said.

CHAPTER 7

THE SHOCK OF seeing Angie was so great that for a moment I felt unsteady on my feet. And then, without either of us seeming to move, she was in my arms. For a time we didn't say a word. We simply held on tight and shut the rest of the world out.

But at last I gently pushed Angie out to arm's length and looked down at her. "Angie, you can't know how much I've wanted to hold you, but nothing has changed. Nothing."

"Maybe, and maybe not."

"What does that mean?"

"I don't know what you'll think about it, Clay, but I spent most of last week in Cheyenne. I went there to see a lawyer someone told me about."

"A lawyer? Why?"

"Because of you. I thought maybe a lawyer could do something. Take Thornton to court, maybe."

"What did the lawyer say?"

She lowered her eyes. "He . . . he wasn't very optimistic. He said what Thornton was doing is clearly illegal, but proving it in court would be another matter."

"Well, so much for that."

"Not necessarily. The lawyer's name is Taminy Kisling, and he has a good reputation. If he takes on a case he does everything in his power to win."

"How does that help me?"

"Well, he wasn't optimistic, but he was interested. He wants to see you."

"How on earth did you know I was here?"

"I didn't. I thought you were gone forever. I came to see Charlie, hoping he might know where you were going. He told me . . ."

I gave Charlie my hardest look. In return he looked sheepish. "I'm sorry, Clay," he said. "Sorry as anything if I did wrong. We were talking and it just slipped out. I'd cut out my tongue before I'd hurt either one of you, doggone it."

"Ah, what the heck, Charlie. It's all right. Forget it. We all let things slip now and then."

I looked back at Angie. "This doesn't change anything," I said. "If I stay here, you'll still be in danger, and nothing on earth is worth getting you hurt or killed. I'm going with Charlie to Alaska."

"At least go see Taminy Kisling before you leave. Tell him your story and listen to what he says."

"It won't help, Angie."

"Maybe not, but isn't it worth trying? Just go talk to him. That's all I ask."

"We aren't leaving for the railroad until day after tomorrow," Charlie said, "and the train won't pull out until Monday. There's plenty of time for you to ride into Cheyenne if you want to go."

I sucked in a chestful of air, let it out slow. "All right, Angie," I said. "I'll ride into Cheyenne and see Kisling. But don't get your hopes up. You said yourself he wasn't very optimistic. It probably won't change anything."

"Even if it doesn't," she said, "at least we'll know we tried. Our love is worth that much, isn't it?"

"You know it is, Angie. Now, so long as we're both here, how about a walk?"

We went outside and spent an hour walking, talking, holding hands, and enjoying the feeling of being together again. But at last it had to end. "If I'm going to make it to Cheyenne and still meet Charlie before the train leaves," I said, "I need to get started."

"We need to get started," she said. "I'm going with you, Clay."

I opened my mouth to argue, closed it without saying a word. Letting Angie go with me was a risk, but not a very large one. Most everyone thought I'd left the country, and besides, I wanted her with me one last time.

I took the time to wash off most of the trail dust and put on better clothes, then we both climbed into her buggy and started down the road. It occurred to me that Angie should stop at home and tell Vance where we were going, but that wasn't in her plans. "If I stop at home," she said, "it will only make Dad worry more. Charlie is going to ride over and tell him I went back to Cheyenne, but he won't mention you."

I didn't like it much, but went along because she was probably right. We hit a rut in the road a mile after leaving Charlie's cabin, and Angie sucked in a sharp breath. I slowed the buggy. "I'm sorry," I said. "I didn't think about your shoulder."

"It's all right. Just a little sore."

I knew from experience that her wound was more than a little sore. It had to be tender as hell.

By the time we'd covered the fifty-odd miles to Cheyenne in the open buggy, we both looked like we'd been on a cattle drive. But without taking the time to clean up, we went to see Taminy Kisling. He looked nothing like the mental image I'd formed of him.

Near as I could remember, I'd never even met a lawyer. I'd certainly never gone to see one for any reason. But like most folks, I imagined how one should look: a thin, balding man with beady eyes and no sense of humor.

Taminy Kisling was three inches over six feet and weighed a solid two-fifteen. He had wide shoulders, big hands, and moved with an easy grace. He was a darkly handsome man with thick, curly black hair. His eyes were slate gray, sharp and knowing.

His office was a finely decorated place. The desk was huge, mahogany, polished to a mirrorlike finish. Bookshelves lined two walls, filled with thick, leather-bound volumes on law, philosophy, and, surprisingly, war.

We shook hands, then sat down. "Now," he said, "I've heard what Miss Douglas had to say. Suppose you tell me the story from your point of view. Begin with the first time you saw Fergus Thornton."

Meeting his gaze, I told my story in as spare a manner as possible, but getting everything important in. When I finished he stood up and walked to a window. For a time he stood there looking out, his big hands locked behind his back. Then he turned to me.

"I would be less than honest if I made you any promises," he said. "Nevertheless, Fergus Thornton is clearly in violation of the law, and I want to help you.

"Technically, what he has done is called inciting to commit murder. Our trouble lies in proving it. Thornton, no doubt, simply told someone of the reward, and they in turn told someone else. Soon it was common knowledge. But unless we can somehow learn the name of the person who heard it from Thornton personally, we have nothing."

"So where does that leave me?"

"Well, if we can get Fergus Thornton to admit placing the bounty on your life, he will have to revoke it, or face prosecution."

"How can we do that?" Angie asked. "I've never met him, but from what Clay tells me, Fergus Thornton is a hard, mean old man."

"Fergus is all that," I said. "And he isn't stupid—he knows better than to admit anything."

Kisling nodded. "Of that I have no doubt," he said. "But I do have an idea. It may not work, but with your permission I'd like to try it."

"What's the idea?" I asked.

"I believe," he said, "we are going to have to kill you."

"What!"

He laughed and said, "We have to make Thornton think you are dead. A lot of details have to be worked out, and even if it works it will be months before you'll be safe. What are your immediate plans?"

I told him about the drive to Alaska.

"My advice is to go ahead with your trip, just as planned. It will give me several months to settle this before you return. In the meantime, do you have any piece of personal property with you that Thornton would recognize?"

I thought about it. "What about my watch? He even tried to buy it from me once."

"Perfect," Kisling said.

After we left his office, Angie asked, "Do you think he can help us?"

"I don't know," I said. "Maybe."

Angie leaned against me. "Even if he doesn't help," she said, "at least we've had this extra time together."

The idea came to me and I spoke before thinking it through. "Angie," I said. "Let's stay here."

"What?"

"Look, if we go back now I'd have to ride like a madman to catch up with the herd. The smart thing for me to do is wait here and catch the train that will pick up the herd, and I can't do that until Monday morning.

"Let's stay in Cheyenne until then. We can get a couple of hotel rooms and use what time we have to see the sights and be together."

"I think that's a wonderful idea, Clay. But why the sudden change of heart? Until this minute it's seemed you couldn't get far enough away from me."

We walked on a few steps, then I stopped and turned to Angie. "I'm not certain," I said. "Maybe it's because Taminy Kisling gave me a little hope. Or maybe I want this time with you, just in case things don't work out."

Angie didn't say a word. She leaned her head against

my chest and we stood like that for a long time, not caring who saw us or what they thought about it.

We did get two hotel rooms, Angie's on the first floor and mine on the third. That night, after shopping for extra clothing, we went to a theater and saw a play. It was fine, but sitting next to Angie is what made the evening special.

The next day we made every effort to see all there was to see in Cheyenne and to forget how few hours we had remaining together. The last thing on earth I wanted to do was leave Angie. I didn't want to go to Alaska, and I didn't even want to think about Fergus Thornton. All I wanted was to stay with Angie and go on feeling as I did right then.

But on Sunday I went to see when the train was coming through that would pick up Charlie and the herd. Not until eight the next morning, I was told, so that gave us one more day together. Instead of spending it sightseeing, we took the buggy and had a picnic. A better day I'd never known.

Angie stayed to see me off next morning, and I boarded the train not knowing if I would ever see her again. Looking back toward the platform as the train pulled away, I watched Angie until she receded from sight.

The train had two passenger cars near the front, a baggage car, then the stock cars and boxcars. I boarded one of the passenger cars, and when the conductor came along asking for tickets I explained about the herd somewhere down the line.

"Technically, I should make you buy a ticket or ride a flatcar until we get there," he said. "But it seems silly to do that when you're going all the way to California. Let's say the first few miles are on the house."

"Thanks. I appreciate it."

I knew Charlie was driving the herd to a site about fifteen miles down the line, but that was all I knew. I expected to find the herd milling around in the open, so it surprised me when the train slowed to a stop in front of two dozen holding pens built in the middle of nowhere.

When I stepped down from the passenger car Charlie and the others were manhandling heavy ramps into position for loading the cattle into the stock cars. Instead of running to help, I leaned against the end of the stock car and rolled a cigarette. It was ten minutes before they got the last ramp into position. I was on my second smoke when Charlie stopped to wipe away sweat, turned, and saw me.

"How long have you been there?" he asked.

"Long enough to avoid what looked like a backbreaking job," I said. "Those ramps look heavy."

Charlie shook his head. "Looks like I'll have to watch you every step of the way," he said. "But I guess I shouldn't complain. I was beginning to think you weren't going to show."

"Didn't make sense to ride all the way back to your ranch when I was already this close." I nodded toward the holding pens. "What is all this?"

"Well, it got so you couldn't get a herd into Cheyenne without running down half a dozen city folks, so a bunch of us ranchers got together and built these pens. This is railroad land, but it's as convenient for them as for us, so they said go ahead and do it."

"Not a bad idea," I said. "Guess we'd best get things moving. But in one way I almost wish I had ridden back. I'm going to miss Apache."

"No you won't," Charlie said. "He's back there with the rest of the horses."

"What? How did you know I wouldn't ride back for him?"

"Didn't. But Angie is a mighty pretty gal, and I had a hunch you'd want to spend as much time with her as you could. So I took a chance and brought your horse."

I laughed. "Guess you know me better than I know myself."

"Nope," Charlie said. "But I do know a bit about pretty women."

There was a twinkle in his eye when he said it, but I had a hunch he was telling the truth. "I'll bet you cut a wide swath when you were young," I said.

"I did all right. Up to the day I met my Colleen. After that she was the only woman in the world for me."

I thought of Angie. "That I can understand. Come on. Let's get those cattle moving. It's a long way to Alaska."

CHAPTER 8

IT WAS SUPPOSED to be roughly a three-day trip to our destination in Sacramento, but on the second day out the boiler split a seam. Fortunately, no one was hurt, but we heard the sound all the way back where we were sitting. It took nine hours to get another engine to us, but truth be told, I was glad to get some fresh air while we waited.

I'd only ridden a train once before, and for a few miles only. I didn't like it that time, either.

The sound of the wheels clickity-clacking against the rails is pleasant enough, and the constant rocking motion makes sleep come easy. But you get a bunch of people in one of those cars and it gets hot, stuffy, and uncomfortable.

Opening the windows gets the air moving and helps, but that also lets smoke and cinders from the engine blow inside the car. The cinders are still hot enough to burn a man, and the smoke makes your eyes water and your throat burn.

All too soon it was time to board the train and leave again. We made it the rest of the way to Sacramento without trouble. After getting the cattle settled in stock pens, we went looking for the ocean. It wasn't hard to find.

Charlie had been this way before, but the rest of us were seeing the ocean for the first time. The feeling was almost indescribable. Even from the shore, there was a feeling of hugeness and tremendous power to all that wide, blue, rolling water.

There was also something fearful about it. Paul Donica and Billy Curtis were standing there beside me, and both of them had the same look on their faces—a mixture of awe and fear. For a time we just stared. Then Billy turned to me. "Can you swim?" he asked.

I shook my head. "Not a lick."

He swallowed hard. "Me neither."

"I can swim," Paul said, "but I sure wouldn't want to try it out there."

Charlie laughed. "This is nothing. Wait till you get out there on a ship. No matter which way you look there's only water, and pretty soon you get to wondering if the captain knows where he's going.

"Then you get to thinking about how deep the water is under you, and wonder how long it would take the boat to sink if something knocked a hole in it. The sailors tell you about sharks big enough to swallow a man whole, and about all kinds of sea serpents. . . . If nothing else, it sure makes Alaska look good when you get there."

"I reckon so," I said. "I reckon so."

There was no telling how long it would take to book passage for us and the cattle, so we found a nice hotel and checked in. We all ate, then Charlie went looking for a ship while the rest of us went to look over the city. We got together again that evening, and Charlie wasn't happy.

"Did you find a ship?" I asked.

"I found two of them," he said. "Being in a hurry means I had to take what was available, and the space is limited. We'll have to divide the cattle into two groups, and split ourselves up as well. I reckon it's best if I take Paul and go on the first ship. Clay, you and Billy will come along a day later. But when we hit Alaska I'll be flat broke. I don't know what we'll do about supplies. It took near every cent I had to get the ships."

"I've got a good bit of money on me," I said. "Let me take care of supplies for the drive."

"I can't ask you to do that, Clay. I'm supposed to pay the bills for those I hire."

"Don't worry about it. You can pay me back when we sell the herd."

"There's a lot that could go wrong," he said. "If we lose the herd you'd be in hot water right along with me."

"If we get in hot water," I said, "we'll take a bath and start over."

Charlie grinned. "All right, then, you've got yourself a deal."

We had a three-day wait for the first ship, and when the time came, we ran the cattle down and loaded them. The sailors and the dock workers paid no attention to the cattle. I asked a sailor about it and he shrugged.

"Mister," he said, "I've spent better than twenty years on the ocean. I been on ships haulin' just about anything you care to name.

"Once we took a whole cargo hold full of maple syrup to a little island in the South Pacific. I been on ships carrying monkeys, camels, and elephants. A bunch of cows don't amount to much after that."

When you looked at it that way, I guess they didn't.

One of us would have to go below deck every day to look after the cattle. We'd brought along barrels of fresh water and a bunch of hay, but the trip was a long one, so both hay and water had to be rationed. The cattle would need a rest and several days of good grazing once we reached Alaska.

The ship was packed top to bottom with cargo and passengers. The cabin they showed Billy and me to was tiny, and we had to share it with three other men. There wasn't enough room in the cabin to change your mind, even when you were alone. I had a hunch the five of us were going to know each other almighty well before we set foot again on dry land.

Then we put out to sea, and before long the last thing on my mind was how many men I shared a cabin with. We hadn't been out of the harbor for more than a few hours when a wind picked up and the ship started bouncing around. My stomach bounced right along with it.

I started to ask Billy if he was feeling queasy, but it wasn't words that tried to come out of my mouth. I made a mad dash for the deck and leaned over the nearest rail, not caring if I fell overboard. I felt like I lost everything I'd eaten for the last three weeks. When at last I raised my head to look around, I saw Billy leaning over the rail only a few feet away. Beyond him a good many other passengers had their own problems.

Billy looked at me and his face was green. "Reckon this can kill a man?" he asked.

"I almost hope it does."

The ship was bouncing, and spray was wetting my face. It tasted of salt. A deckhand went walking by and I grabbed his arm. "How long do you expect this storm will last?" I asked.

A surprised look came over his face and he looked out at the water. "Huh, what storm?"

Swallowing hard, I waved a hand toward the ocean. "*This* storm."

"Mister, meaning nothing personal, but I don't know what you're talking about. This is perfect sailing weather. If we're lucky this weather will hold all the way to port. We might run into a storm, but there's no sign of one that I can see."

He walked off, shaking his head. Billy looked at me, and his face had gone from green to pure white. "Did he say this weather would hold all the way if we're lucky?"

Afraid to risk speaking again, I just nodded. Then my head went back over the rail.

By the next day we'd found our sea legs, as one sailor put it, and after that we were able to hold things down. But I didn't eat enough to keep a bird alive for the rest of the trip, and nothing ever looked so good as that first sight of land at the end of our journey.

Skagway had enough water in its harbor to let the big steamship get right up to a dock, and no sooner did it get there than people went to work unloading cargo. But not before I jumped ship. I didn't care about the cargo, the other passengers, or even the cattle. After close to three weeks aboard ship, I just wanted solid ground under my feet as quickly as possible.

Billy was right behind me, and we both saw Charlie and Paul coming through the crowd at the same time. Charlie was wearing a smile that went from ear to ear. A cloud of blue smoke from his pipe filled the air around him, and when he was close enough, he jabbed the stem of his pipe toward the ocean. "Well," he asked, "how did you like traveling by ship?"

"Charlie," I said, "right now I don't know whether I should shake your hand or hit you square on the nose."

"Don't tell me," he said, "that a big, strong, young fellow like you had the same kind of trouble poor Paul had?"

"If you mean did I spend the first day and a half leaning over the rail to feed the fish, then the answer is yes. You old coot, why didn't you warn us about that?"

"Never crossed my mind," he said. "Never happened to me personal. Guess some of us are born sailors, and others are landlubbers through and through."

Not being able to think of a suitable reply to that remark, I let it pass and looked around. Skagway seemed to have almost as many people as it had space to put them. As far as I could see, which wasn't all that far, people swarmed like ants scurrying for the last crumb of food at a picnic. I commented on it to Charlie.

"Took me by surprise, too," he said. "Last time I was up here this place had about two buildings and ten men to fill them.

"Fellow I talked to this morning told me someone tried to count the folks here and quit at ten thousand. He allowed there might be half again as many, but they come and go so fast that nobody really knows.

"Anyway, it's certain sure there's enough to jam the passes. Let's get our horses and take care of the cattle, then we'll find someplace where we can eat."

The horses had come in on the same ship that brought Charlie, and he'd put them up at a corral almost a half mile away. They'd already found a good site for the cattle and had half the herd already there and grazing. It was well outside of town, and Charlie had hired an out-of-money gold seeker to watch them.

You'd think driving cattle through the congested streets of Skagway would be a problem, but people were so intent on getting set to tackle the goldfields beyond the mountains that they seemed unaware of anything else, including fifty-odd cattle coming down the street. Men would side-step when they had to, but for the most part the cattle had to make way for the men, rather than the other way around.

We had three or four cantankerous bulls in that bunch, and I sat light in the saddle, ready to cut them back into the herd if they took a notion to see how far they could knock somebody, but it seemed I was worried about nothing. The cattle just wanted out of town and went where we pointed them.

When we had all the cattle together, Charlie introduced me to the fellow he'd hired to watch over them. His name was Jamie Scott. Twenty-nine years old, he was slim to the point of being skinny and about two inches under six feet. His hair was a sandy brown, and his clothing was well past the stage where it should have been thrown away.

I asked how long he'd been in Alaska, and he shook his head slowly. "Too long," he said. "Too damn long. I came in last year, and all I want now is to get out. I got me a nice little farm back in Ohio, and I've a wife and two kids waiting there. I never should have left, but I got to reading the newspaper stories about how the gold up here was just lying there on the ground begging to be picked up, and I couldn't wait to get up here."

"You going home?" I asked.

"The moment I get passage money. Anybody ever mentions gold or Alaska to me again is going to get an ax handle bounced off his head."

With the cattle happily chewing away at the first good grass they'd seen in too long, and with Jamie left to watch them, the rest of us started back into Skagway. As we rode along, Charlie talked to us. "You've never seen a place like Skagway," he said. "I been around a long time, and I've seen a lot, but there's never been a town like this.

"There ain't a con game known to man that you can't find being worked, and folks are coming up with new ones every day. You'll just have to watch yourselves on most of them, but I will tell you this—if anybody offers to sell you a map of the best packing trails for a dollar, get away from him fast. The moment you pull out your wallet someone will knock you down and take it.

"And stay away from a gambling house called Jeff's Place. It's owned by a fellow called Soapy Smith, and he runs most of the crooked things in Skagway. They say he has a hundred men working for him, and every last one of them would steal his own mother's last dollar. If a fellow asks if you'd like to telegraph back home to let folks know you made it here safe and sound, you can bet that fellow works for Soapy."

"How do you figure that?" Billy asked. "Sending a telegram sounds like a good idea. My folks might be worried."

"It is a fine idea," Charlie said, "except for one thing. Telegraph wires haven't been strung yet, and won't be for years. There's a telegraph office, all right, and they'll tap out a message for you. A few hours later you'll even get a reply . . . for another five dollars.

"But if you follow the wires, you'll find they end about

two hundred yards away. The whole thing is a front, but they tell me Soapy is making a killing."

"You mentioned money," I said, "and that reminds me. How much do you think the supplies will cost?"

"Prices in Skagway are higher than a Boston girl's nose," he said, "but we ain't lookin' for gold, so we won't need much in the way of an outfit. We need flour, sugar, coffee, salt pork, and a few odds and ends. And we'll need a bit of trail gear and maybe a few other things. Throw in a good pack mule, and I think we can get it all for three hundred or so. Can you swing that much?"

I counted out five hundred dollars and handed it to Charlie. "If that isn't enough," I said, "I have a bit more."

"If it takes more than this, I've lost my touch. Now let's hunt some food."

CHAPTER 9

WE FOUND A restaurant that had enough room for the four of us to sit together, and ordered our food. While we were eating, a hard-eyed man of about fifty walked by our table, glanced at us, and started to go on. Then he looked harder and stopped. "Charlie Slaughter, is it you hiding under that hat?"

Charlie looked up, stared at the man a moment, then smiled and whooped. "Well, I'll be danged. Hank Criswell. I thought you went back to the States right after I did."

"I went back, all right, but I couldn't stay away. I kept reading stories about all the gold they're finding, and it got to me. Looks like you couldn't stay away, either. Ain't you getting a little old in the tooth to go hunting gold?"

"Hell," Charlie said, "I ain't much older'n you. And I ain't up here hunting gold. I brought my gold with me."

"If you did that," Hank said, "then you're one up on all the rest of us."

"Pull up a chair," Charlie said, "and I'll tell you all about it."

Hank found a chair and slid it into place between me and Paul. Charlie made quick work of telling him the story. Hank shook his head. "Was that your cattle that come through town today? I might expect a plan like that from a bunch of cheechakos like these boys, but an old sourdough like you should know better. If there was any way in hell of getting cattle across the Chilkoot or through White Pass, it would have been done long ago. I can't think of anyone who's been fool enough to even try it."

"If they haven't tried," I asked, "how do they know it can't be done?"

"You wouldn't ask that if you'd seen those passes up close. Guess you'll have to learn the hard way. Cheechakos always do. But I'm surprised at you, Charlie."

"That's twice you've called us cheechakos," Billy said. "I don't know what it means, but I don't think I like the sound of it."

"I meant no offense," Hank said. "A cheechako is someone who's here for the first time. Spend a winter in the interior, come back out alive, and you're a sourdough."

Charlie took a bite of meat, chewed and swallowed, then wiped his mouth. "Hank, I've spent better than two years thinking about this, and I think we can do it. I know we can't get the cattle over the Chilkoot. A lot of men can't make that climb. But I think there's a good chance of getting them through White Pass."

"Have you been through White Pass?"

Charlie nodded. "Went through it my first time here. I made it, all right."

"What were you riding?"

"Nothing. I went through on foot. But there's been plenty of mules taken through White Pass."

Hank took a plug of tobacco from his pocket and bit off a jawful. He worked it into a lather and spit a stream of brown juice toward a spittoon. About half made it in.

"Charlie, White Pass is thirty-four miles of rough trail, and eleven miles of pure hell. You go through on foot and it ain't so bad, but it's hell on horses and mules. Folks have named that eleven-mile stretch Dead Horse Trail, and they're talking about closing it down because of the stench."

"What stench?" Paul asked.

"The stench from the dead horses and mules that fall off the trail and into the valley below. Somebody counted near a thousand carcasses over that stretch, with more dying every day."

Charlie nodded. "That's true enough," he said, "but you can blame most of that on the people rather than the animals. The damn fools load down a mule with so much gear it can barely walk, then they try to take it through White Pass. It's a wonder any of them make it through.

"Cattle ain't as sure-footed as mules, but they won't be carrying anything. We'll have to take them through the rougher stretches a few at a time, and we may lose a couple, but we'll make it in with most of them."

"I got my doubts," Hank said, "but if you do get them through, you'll be a well-off man. A man could trade a prime steak for an ounce of gold up to Dawson."

"Dawson? I was planning on pushing them to Forty Mile."

"Then you haven't heard?"

"I reckon not," Charlie said. "Heard what?"

"About the big strike at Dawson. Folks are flocking in, and they say it's the biggest payoff yet. You won't have to change your route, neither. Dawson is maybe fifty miles this side of Forty Mile Creek."

"They'll be wantin' beef," Charlie said, "and they'll pay to get it."

Hank spat again. "Yes, sir, that's a fact. Man gets tired of sourdough pancakes and potatoes after a time. Let him live like that for a couple of months, and he'd give a week's wages to sink his choppers into a steak. Yes, sir, you get them cattle through, and you can name your own price."

"There's something I don't understand," Billy said. "Why don't they go out and shoot their own meat? Ain't there no wild game in Alaska?"

Hank grunted. "Son, we got more wild game here than all the outside United States put together. We got white bears, black bears, and brown bears. We got moose, deer, beaver, and something called caribou that run in herds like buffalo used to out on the plains.

"You ask Charlie about the wild game to be had. He's seen it all and et most of it."

"Then why don't the miners shoot their own meat?"

"Because this country is big," Charlie said, "and she's wild. Half the miners couldn't find a moose in a strawberry patch, and a lot of the others couldn't hit one with a rifle from ten feet. Besides, owning a gold claim kind of ties a man down. Step one foot off it and somebody else is liable to jump on. Gold fever has killed more men than cholera. Show a man a few flakes of color in a stream and he gets the sickness. After that he'd sit and starve before he'd go off hunting game."

Hank stood up. "Well, I got to find me a couple of cheap working men with good backs to get my supplies over the Chilkoot. You boys take care, and I wish you luck."

"Why not throw in with us?" Charlie asked. "We could use another good man."

Hank shook his head. "Thanks for the offer, but bad as the Chilkoot is, White Pass is worse. Just the thought of trying to get through there with a bunch of knothead cattle gives me the willies. We might meet up on the other side of the mountains, though, if we both make it through. If you still need a hand then, I'll be glad to lend it."

He started to turn away, stopped, and looked back. "You likely already know it," he said, "but there's plenty of talk going on about them cattle of yours. Might be best if you all slept with them."

"What have you heard?" I asked.

He shrugged. "Nothing specific. But there's a thousand men in this town who'd shoot a man for a pocket-worn nickel. Those cattle are worth ten times as much on the other side of the mountains, but they're worth a-plenty on this side."

"Thanks," I said. "We'll watch them close."

Hank looked me over closer than he had before. "I reckon you will," he said.

For a time we sat quiet, thinking about what Hank had told us. Trouble was, I had no way of judging his words. I needed to see the country firsthand. I needed to saddle Apache and ride through White Pass without worrying about cattle. It was the only way to understand the problems facing us.

"Charlie," I asked, "when did you have in mind to pull out?"

He rubbed his jaw whiskers. "Not for a few days. Might even wait a week. Traveling by train and ship is hard on cattle. They could use a few days to rest and fatten up. Next Monday, say?"

"Think you can hold things down around here without me for a time?"

"Don't see why not. Where you going?"

I told him about wanting to ride through White Pass. "I don't doubt your word at all," I said. "But if I can take a look at things for myself, I'll be able to see problems before they come."

Charlie took out his pipe and tamped tobacco into the bowl. "Not a bad idea, that," he said. "You want I should come along?"

"No, sir. I'd rather you didn't. Be best if I look at things without anyone along to influence my thoughts."

He nodded. "All right. When you leaving?"

"Tomorrow, I guess. Not too early."

"Good enough. I'll start hunting supplies and be ready to pull out when you get back."

We left the restaurant, going through a thick crowd of men just coming in. After walking around for a while to see the sights, Billy and Paul went back to help watch over the cattle. Charlie went to start making deals for supplies, and I was left on my own.

Stopping in at a mercantile, I bought a tin coffee cup

for two bits. Then I went into the first restaurant I came to and held out the cup to a man wearing a dirty apron. "How about filling that up for me?" I asked.

"Cost you a nickel," he said.

I gave him a nickel, so he took the cup and filled it to the rim with hot coffee. I went back outside and set the cup down long enough to roll a smoke, then picked it up, and walked down to the docks.

You never saw a busier bunch of people than the fellows unloading those steamships. They'd run out of room to stack things long before, so they'd started stacking this on top of that, and that on top of this. The entire dock area was a mass of jumbled cargo, and dozens, maybe hundreds of men were digging through it, looking for some particular piece of freight they were expecting.

The captain of one of the steamships was standing on deck with his arms crossed, looking down at a man on the dock who was wearing a black suit that had seen its better days long ago. He was yelling at the captain.

"I tell you, I'm a doctor," he was saying. "If I don't find those supplies, a lot of men might die."

The captain had gray, bushy sideburns and a face reddened by too much alcohol. "The best thing that could happen to this godforsaken place would be a lot of men dying," he yelled back. "If you want your cargo that much, you should have been here when it was unloaded."

"But your men unloaded the ship. Surely they know where I can find it."

"Look, sir," the captain yelled. "My duty is to get anything and everything on my ship to port safely. I have done that. What happens to cargo after it leaves my ship does not concern me. Now good day, sir."

The captain turned and walked away, leaving the frustrated doctor standing there. He looked around with a bewildered expression on his face. My coffee was half gone and getting cold. I tossed it out of the cup and into the water. "If you'll tell me what to look for," I said, "I'll try to help you find it."

His face brightened. "Would you, sir? That's very good of you."

"Got nothing better to do," I said. "Exactly what are we looking for?"

"Well, as I said, it's a crate. I'm not sure of the size, maybe four feet to the side. It should be clearly marked in red letters."

Now, you'd think finding a four-foot-square crate marked "Medical Supplies" in big red letters would be easy to find, but in that jumble it was like looking for a needle in a haystack. We asked anyone who would listen to keep watch for it as they dug for their own freight, but it still took the better part of an hour before a fellow yelled out that he'd uncovered it.

Someone had gone to the expense of having a buggy shipped up, and a fine, fancy thing it was. Only it was completely covered by shipping crates. The leather on the seat was torn, one spoke was broken, and it was filthy. The crate we were looking for was on the buggy's seat and was probably responsible for the split leather.

The crate must have weighed close to two hundred pounds, but most of the weight was in the wood itself. Prying off the lid with a borrowed crowbar, we dug through the wadded up paper used as packing and found three boxes of medical supplies. They weighed about twenty-five pounds each. "Do you need help getting them back to your office?"

"Thank you, no," he said. "I believe I can handle them from here. I want to thank you for your help. What do I owe you?"

"Nothing at all," I said. "Glad to help."

"That's very decent of you. My name is Jonas Carlyle. Come by my office sometime and I'll give you a physical. No charge, of course."

He wandered back toward the center of town, staggering a little under the weight of the supplies, and I shook my head. I'd been offered payment for helping folks before, but nobody had ever offered to poke and prod my body. No doubt about it, I had to be more careful choosing who to help.

I walked on down the beach, and after a bit I heard the sound of dogs barking. There was nothing unusual about that, Skagway had dogs running all over, but this sounded like a lot of dogs, all unhappy about something. As I came closer to the sound, I realized the barking was coming from crated animals. An entire section of the beach was filled with wooden cages, each holding at least one dog. Some cages held a dozen or more.

You never saw such a bunch of dogs in your life. The cages held huge dogs, tiny dogs, and everything in between. Colors varied even more than size, starting at snow white and ending with pure black.

A rough-dressed fellow carrying a club saw me looking and came over. "One of them yours?" he asked.

"No, sir. Just looking. What in the world do people want with all these dogs?"

"Damn fools bring them in to pull sleds," he said. "Horses ain't much good up here in the winter, so folks travel by dogsled. Works real well, too.

"Trouble is, there ain't near enough dogs in Alaska to go around, so folks buy 'em from the States, sight unseen. There's a bunch of folks back there gettin' rich shipping dogs up here, but not one dog in ten is any good for hauling a heavy sled. Hell, some of these dogs ain't big enough to pull a dead cat across the yard. Others ain't got enough hair to keep 'em warm now, let alone in a blizzard.

"No, sir. It takes a big, strong-built dog with thick fur to get through the winter here. Near all of these mutts will be dead long before spring."

Something growled deeply in a large crate nearby, and

I walked over to it. "You be careful of that one, mister," the man said. "I've seen some big, wicked-looking dogs in my time here, but I've never seen one bigger or meaner looking than that fellow."

Kneeling down, I looked through the slats. The dog inside must have weighed close to two-hundred pounds, most of it in the huge muscles of the shoulders and neck. The head was huge and the mouth filled with teeth that looked capable of snapping a man's hand off at the wrist.

"What kind of dog is he?" I asked.

"I ain't sure. I think the bill of lading says he's a mastiff, whatever that is. I'd sure enough bet on him being alive when spring comes. Hell, any bear with a brain would run from that dog."

Keeping my hand below the level of his head and my fingers spread wide, I slowly reached between the slats of the cage. The dog growled, bared his fangs. "Mister, you'd best not mess with that dog. He'll have your arm for supper."

My fingers touched fur, began to slowly stroke. The dog never completely stopped growling, but he did sniff my hand. I talked to him as I petted, and soon we were fast friends.

"You're either braver or dumber than I am, friend," the man said. "I wouldn't have tried that for a pound of gold dust."

"I like dogs," I said. "We get along."

After a bit I went back into town and bought what things I would need for my ride through White Pass. Then I rode back out to the herd. Charlie hadn't returned, but the others were there, and they expected trouble.

CHAPTER 10

IT WAS TWO hours or so before dark, and the boys had a fire going and coffee on when I rode up. Paul and Jamie were out riding slow around the cattle to keep them calm, but Billy was sitting near the fire, holding a cup of coffee. He had a rifle close at hand.

"I was hoping you'd get back," he said. "Looks like somebody wants to keep an eye on the herd."

"What makes you think so?"

Billy never moved anything except his eyes. "See that big outcropping of gray rock about three hundred yards straight out from where my horse is standing?"

"I see it."

"If you look real close you'll see a slab of rock with a reddish tint to it over near the left side. Don't look right at it, but watch it casual-like for a few minutes."

Pouring myself a cup of coffee, I sat down and put my back against a log. I made sure to sit where I could watch the slab of rock. Nothing happened for three minutes, then sunlight glinted off something behind the rock.

"Did you see it?" Billy asked.

"Uh-huh. Any idea what it is?"

"I know what it is," Billy said. "It's a man watching us through some kind of spyglass. Saw him sneakin' in there better'n an hour ago."

"Was he carrying a rifle?"

Billy took a drink of coffee. "Couldn't tell. Don't think so, but I just couldn't tell."

For twenty minutes we sat there, and I ran through every possibility I could think of. It might be nothing to worry about. It might be someone watching us just in case we eased up and he got a chance to steal something. Or it might be someone was watching us until a few friends showed up to take the herd away from us.

Whatever the man was doing there, it was certain he was up to no good. The thing to do was prepare for the worst. If it didn't happen we'd have wasted a little time, and if it did happen we'd be ready.

Billy had the fire going in a good spot, with several large boulders nearby to keep off the wind and two large logs to lean against or sit on. The cattle were grazing in a meadow that ended against a bluff on one side and a tree-choked draw on the other. If they should stampede it would likely be back toward us.

It was possible that whoever was out there planned to wait until well into the night, then start the cattle running our way, maybe hoping some or all of us would be killed. But he'd have to know some cattle might be lost that way, and they were worth too much money alive.

My bet was the fellow out there had friends, and he was watching us until they arrived later in the night. Or perhaps even the next night. If I was wanting to steal a herd of cattle under these conditions, I'd put someone out to watch them until the time was right, and I had to believe they would do the same.

As I was sitting there thinking over the possibilities and watching the man out yonder, Charlie came riding up with two pack mules in tow behind him. Both mules were loaded to the hilt with supplies.

"Looks like you found what you needed," I said.

Charlie grinned. "Got everything but the perishables, and I got it for a song. Young fellow had all this bought and paid for, and tried to take it over the Chilkoot. He got about halfway up with the first load, thought about how many times he was going to have to climb that mountain to get everything over, and decided he didn't want to be a gold miner after all."

"Too bad," I said. "He made a long trip up here for nothing."

Charlie grunted. "Better for us," he said, "and better for him. If he quit that easy he'd never have lasted out the winter."

Standing up, I began helping Charlie unload the mules, and as we worked I quietly told him about the man watching us. Charlie frowned. "Kinda thought somebody'd make a play," he said. "I did hope they'd wait until we got through White Pass. You got any ideas?"

"Not really, you?"

"Just one," he said.

"Let's hear it."

Charlie pulled his rifle out of the scabbard. It was a Winchester lever-action, chambered for the new 30–30 cartridge. He jacked a round into the chamber and winked at me. "Get ready. This might cause some trouble."

"Let her rip," I said.

Charlie brought the rifle to his shoulder and started firing. The first bullet spanged off the top of the red rock; the second went over the top and hit a bigger rock farther back, kicking up rock dust and ricocheting away with an ugly sound. He fired twice more, and on the last bullet a man came out from behind the rock, running straight away, looking like a mountain goat as he went over country rough enough to stop a mule.

"Whooee, look at him go," Billy said. "Reckon that'll teach him a lesson."

"It might just teach him not to be seen next time," I said, "but it was worth the try."

"What now?" Billy asked.

"Now we keep up our guard and wait," I said. "Not much else we can do."

Charlie spat. "If trouble does come," he said, "I'd rather

it happen when my belly's full. Help me unpack and I'll put supper on."

We dug out the food Charlie had brought, and he went to work. Picking up the coffeepot, I found it was nearly empty. Taking it down to a nearby stream, I filled it with water for another pot, then washed my face and hands. It was May, and the water coming down from the mountains was still ice-cold. It felt fine.

Charlie's supper consisted of fried potatoes, sourdough bread, and a ten-pound hunk of roasted moose meat he'd bought in Skagway. It wasn't fancy, but it was filling. I ate, poured a cup of coffee, and drank it in the saddle while Billy and I rode out to relieve Paul and Jamie.

Darkness fell, and with it a moon came from behind the mountains. It wasn't full, but between it and the stars there was enough light to see fairly well. Billy walked his horse in a circle around the herd in one direction, and I rode in the other. We sang in a low voice to let the cattle know who we were, and after about three hours of this we stopped and talked for a minute.

"Everything seems quiet enough," Billy said. "Might be nothing will happen tonight."

"Suits me. I like it quiet."

"Cold, though," he said. "Mighty cold for May."

"Guess it takes a while for summer to come up in this country. It is cold, at that."

"Give me your cup and I'll ride back to camp. If there's coffee I'll bring you a cup."

"Sounds good. Thanks."

I gave Billy my cup, and he walked his horse back toward camp. We had the fire built two hundred yards from the herd, and Billy faded into the darkness long before he'd traveled that far. Clicking my tongue and touching Apache lightly with a spur, I started another go-round of the herd. Halfway around, I heard something.

It wasn't much of a sound, and it wasn't close. Stopping

Apache, I strained my ears into the darkness. All I heard were cattle lowing, a bull walking through grass nearby, some kind of night bird calling in the distance . . . nothing out of the ordinary.

I was about to start Apache moving when I heard the sound again. It was the creaking kind of sound saddle leather makes when a man shifts his weight. Next came what I knew had to be a horseshoe striking a stone.

A cloud drifted over the moon and darkness closed in around me. At least one rider was out there and moving my way. It wasn't Billy returning with coffee, because of the direction.

A leather thong held the Colt in my holster, and I slipped it off. A minute passed, then another. Somebody coughed softly, saddle leather creaked, a horse whinnied. Then the moon came out from behind the clouds and there they were, four men riding ten feet apart, walking their horses right toward me.

We saw each other at the same time. One of them whipped up a rifle and fired, the muzzle blast like a sun bursting in the night. Something snapped through the air near me, and then my own Colt was out. I fired twice, ramming my spurs into Apache's ribs on the first shot. He jumped and went into a run like a scared rabbit.

Running would only get me a bullet in the back, so I charged Apache right into them. I fired again at a distance of no more than five feet and a man screamed. Guns were hammering, Apache hit another horse head on and both horses went down.

Kicking free of the stirrups so Apache wouldn't roll on me, I hit the ground hard enough to knock the air from my lungs. Another cloud went over the moon and darkness closed in. Horses stomped all around me, and I fired at a shape in the night. Two rifles fired back and something hot singed my ear.

More rifles were shattering the night in the distance,

and then somebody not far off swore. "Damn it," he said. "This ain't going right. Let's get out of here."

My Colt was empty and I reloaded it by feel. Hoofbeats hammered the ground, faded into the distance. Two more rifle shots sounded from the direction of the camp, then silence filled the night.

The cattle were milling about, threatening to stampede, but as nothing else happened, they slowly calmed down. Getting to my feet, I walked back toward the camp, keeping my Colt in my hand. My shoulder hurt and my knee felt skinned, but I didn't stop to take account of my injuries. A cow walked in front of me and I smacked it lightly on the rump. It moved quickly on.

The fire was nothing but a faintly glowing bed of coals, and I stopped thirty yards away. I could see nothing. A yell might draw a shot, but walking in from the night without yelling would surely get me killed. "Charlie, you boys all right?"

"It's all right," Charlie yelled back. "They took off like rabbits when the shooting started."

Walking on toward the camp, I saw somebody move near the coals, then the fire flared to life as an armload of wood was dropped on the hot coals. Light spread from the fire and I holstered my Colt. Billy picked two tin cups from the ground and filled them with coffee that had been simmering on the hot coals. He handed one cup to me. "Here's your coffee," he said.

Taking the cup, I sat down on a log, sipped the coffee. It was strong enough to strip paint. Setting the cup down, I rolled a smoke and lit it with a stick from the fire. Charlie poured himself a cup and sat down near me. "We got lucky," he said. "Plain damn lucky. Billy woke me and Paul up getting coffee, else those boys would have caught us sleeping."

"Wasn't enough light from the fire to see a thing," Billy said. "I tripped over something and fell right across Charlie's legs. He woke up cursing, and that brought Paul awake. Somebody out there must have panicked at the sound of our voices and started shooting too soon. We shot back, aiming at the muzzle flashes."

"It could've been worse," Charlie said.

Paul came walking over to us, his face pale in the firelight. "Jamie's dead," he said.

"Ah, hell," Charlie said.

We walked over to Jamie's blankets. A bullet had torn through his blankets and caught him in the center of the back. "Must have been from that first shot," Paul said. "Like as not, Jamie never knew what hit him."

"All he wanted to do was get out and go home," Billy said. "Back to his family in Ohio."

"Soapy Smith is behind this," Charlie said. "Nobody would dare trying something like this less'n he said so."

"Come morning," I said, "we'll ride in and see what he has to say for himself."

"Soapy has a hundred men working for him," Charlie said. "That's a lot to handle."

"There's only one of him," I said. "And that's who we'll be talking to."

CHAPTER 11

SLEEP WAS A long time coming that night, and when at last it did come, my dreams were of guns hammering in the night and of Jamie lying dead beneath his blankets. It was the first time in weeks I hadn't dreamed of Angie.

Clouds moved in during the night, and with the clouds came more cold. It was snowing when we woke up, and for a time I stayed in my blankets, shivering, but unwilling to uncover myself long enough to rebuild the fire. Just as I finally found the courage to get up, Billy rolled from his blankets and started throwing wood on the fire.

"If you'd waited another thirty seconds," I said, "I would have been up."

Billy's teeth were chattering. "N . . n . . now you . . t . . t . . tell me."

I rolled out anyway, and went for a fresh coffeepot of water. The snow wasn't coming down heavy, but it was sticking to the grass and threatening to pile up some. If it snowed too much it could threaten our plans for driving the cattle through White Pass.

Charlie was sitting up and looking around when I came back with the coffee water. "You've been up here before," I said. "Do you think we're in for it?"

"The snow, you mean?" He sniffed the air. "There's no tellin' for sure, but I'd bet against it. She just don't smell like a real storm."

Charlie was the cook in the outfit, and he made short work of fixing breakfast once Billy had a good fire going. Paul rode out right after breakfast to find Apache. He came back a half hour later, Apache trotting along behind him.

"There's a dead man out there," he said to me. "Looks like you made up for Jamie."

"Not hardly," I said.

Then we buried Jamie Scott. All he had on him was a pocket watch, three dollars in change, and a half dozen letters from his wife. The watch had a picture of him and his family on the inside of the case. His wife was a plainly attractive woman with brown hair and knowing eyes. I kept his belongings to send to her.

I had a Bible in my saddlebags, and when the dirt was patted down over Jamie's grave, I opened it up and said a few words.

Afterward, I took Apache and one of the pack mules out to where John found the dead man. He was lying on his stomach and I rolled him over. He looked to be part Indian, but he had a thick, long beard that my bullet had parted the hard way, nicking his chin and angling over to slice his jugular vein.

A mule isn't nearly as skittish as a horse under most conditions, but that one shied some at the smell of blood. With some talking, patting, and a firm hand, he held still enough for me to get the body over his back and lash it in place. When I rode back to camp with that body over the mule's back, Paul, Billy, and Charlie all stood up to watch me come. "Ought to've left him there," Charlie said. "Wolves got to eat just like people."

"You said Soapy Smith likely sent this fellow out here. I mean to give him back."

Charlie grinned. "Kerrigan, you do play rough. Soapy ain't gonna like that. Make him look bad."

"I don't give a damn what he likes," I said. "I've a message for him, and I want it to come through loud and clear."

"Let's saddle the horses," Billy said. "I wouldn't miss this for all the gold in Alaska."

We rode into Skagway four abreast. Folks looked once, then twice. On the second look they moved aside and headed off the streets and into the nearest business. "They smell trouble," Charlie said.

Charlie led the way to Jeff's Place, and we slid off our horses. Slipping the knot that held the dead man on the mule, I dropped him over my shoulder and went into the saloon. Early as it was, the place was smoke-filled and crowded. The building was alive with the sound of laughing, swearing, and idle conversation, but when folks saw that body over my shoulder they went quiet.

Men stepped aside to let us through, but a lot of them didn't look the least bit frightened. They all wore guns. "That's Soapy sittin' there at the corner table," Charlie said.

Soapy was sitting with his back to the wall, and two burly, rough-dressed fellows sat on either side of him. Walking over to the table, I dropped the body across it. The body was too long for the table and the feet caught one of the men on the shoulder, almost knocking him off his chair.

Catching his balance, the man came to his feet. "What the hell do you think—"

That was as far as he got. I caught him on the chin with a good right hand and he hit on his shoulders. He groaned, but I knew he'd be out of it for some time.

Soapy Smith was a tall, thin, handsome man with a black, neatly trimmed beard. "What is this?" he asked.

"It's a dead man," I said. "You've seen them before."

"Why bring him to me?"

"Because him and a few others tried to steal our cattle last night, and they tell me you run every crooked angle in this town."

"People exaggerate. I'm an upstanding citizen."

"Sure you are," I said. Leaning over the table, I put my face close to his. "But if you bother those cattle, I'll kill you, or die trying. That's just the way it is."

He smiled, but there was no humor in it. "I'm sure your cattle are quite safe," he said. "Besides, I'm curious to see if you can get those cattle through White Pass. Men are betting against it."

"Take all the bets you can get," I said. "We're going to make it."

"All right. Anything else?"

"As a matter of fact," I said, "there is. A good man was killed out there last night, and he had a family back in Ohio. Being the generous, upstanding citizen you claim to be, you might make a contribution to his family. Say, five hundred dollars."

Soapy's face turned a shade lighter. "That's a lot of money, even in Alaska."

I just looked at him. He reached inside his jacket. The sound of my Colt clearing leather and cocking was loud in the hush of the saloon. Soapy never even blinked.

"Just reaching for my wallet," he said.

Using two fingers, he took a wallet from a pocket in his jacket and counted out the money. I picked it up and slipped it into a pocket of my own. "That squares us for now," I said.

With Charlie and the others watching my back, I turned and started for the door. "What's your name?" Soapy called.

Stopping, I looked back at him. "It's Kerrigan."

"Fine, Kerrigan. Your cattle will be safe. It took courage to walk in here, and I appreciate courage. But if you do get the cattle through White Pass, well, you understand I can't promise what will happen on the other side. My influence only extends so far."

I nodded and walked outside. Charlie and the others

came out behind me. "You scared him," Paul said. "He'll leave us alone."

"I didn't scare him," I said. "Not even a little bit. Now he has to get even, or folks won't pay any attention to him. But at least he knows we won't go down easy, so maybe it will be a while before he tries anything else."

"You were right to stand up to him. He would have tried again anyway," Charlie said. "If we get those cattle through White Pass they'll be worth a hundred thousand dollars, and Soapy ain't about to let that kind of money get away."

"Well, keep your eyes open and a rifle close to hand while I'm gone."

I felt a thousand pairs of eyes on us as we walked through Skagway.

We went to the bank, where I turned the five hundred dollars into a bank draft. I wrote a short letter and posted everything to go out on the next ship to Jamie's widow.

It wasn't much, but it was all I could do. Many a man has died without half that being done for his family, and when my time came, I hoped someone would take the time to do the same for me.

We rode back to our camp. Two inches of fresh snow covered the ground, but no more was coming down and the sky was clearing. I picked up a couple of things for my ride through White Pass. While Charlie told me what to watch for in White Pass, I loaded my gear onto Apache.

I headed out. The pass started right outside of Skagway, and even a tenderfoot could have found it by the almost unbroken stream of cheechakos constantly starting along the trail. Most went on foot, leading pack mules behind them, but here and there I saw someone on horseback.

There were stretches of the pass that a man could take at a gallop, and other places where Apache had to walk slow and choose his footing with care. I'd been over some rough trails before, though, and didn't see why cattle couldn't make it over this one. Then I came to the eleven-mile section known as Dead Horse Trail.

It was a nightmare. In long stretches the trail was nothing more than a few feet of rock above a long drop. In other long stretches, deep mire and snow sucked in man and beast three feet or more. Men cursed fallen mules; two horses slipped off the edge of the trail and joined hundreds of other rotting carcasses in the valley below.

The air was rank, filled with the stench of rotting animals, and before the second day of my ride was over I knew I was in trouble. On the third day I had to work my way across an avalanche covering the trail. That entire day I covered three miles.

I was twelve days getting through the pass and back to our camp, and at that, I hadn't even gone all the way to the other side. Dropping wearily to the ground near the fire, I gratefully accepted the plate of food and cup of coffee Billy handed me. "Well," Charlie asked, "what do you think?"

I ate the big chunk of sourdough bread and scraped the plate clean before answering. "I don't know," I said. "We may not make it at all, and if we do it'll take us a month, maybe longer. And we're sure going to lose some cattle. I don't know, Charlie. There's a few spots where we'll have to take them through a head at a time, and at least a dozen other stretches where we can't let more than a dozen or so go through at once."

Charlie shook his head. "I just don't remember it being that bad," he said. "Maybe I am getting old."

Bumming tobacco and papers off Paul, I rolled a smoke and lit it. "In the last twelve days I've seen horses and mules fall to their deaths," I said, "not to mention the ones with broken legs that had to be shot. I will say this, Charlie. You were right about one thing. A lot of those horses and mules were loaded down so heavy they could barely walk on level ground."

Charlie nodded. "Did you see even one unloaded horse or mule fall?"

I thought back. "No, sir, I didn't. A few men unloaded their pack mules and carried the equipment across the really bad spots. I can't remember any of those mules falling."

He poured a cup of coffee. "Never figured on you being gone as long as you were," he said, "but I'm glad you went over the trail. If you say we can't make it, Kerrigan, I'll sell the cattle right here in Skagway."

My coffee was cold. Dumping it on the ground, I refilled the cup, sipped. It was scalding hot. "Let's give it a try," I said. "If things get too bad we can always turn around and come back."

Charlie whooped. "That's what I wanted to hear," he said. "When do we leave?"

"Bright and early tomorrow. Today I plan to take it easy and get caught up on my eating."

"Good enough," Charlie said. "I need to pick up the perishables we'll need anyway."

It had been midmorning when I rode back into camp, and rest and food was all I cared about at the time. But when Charlie saddled his horse to ride into Skagway about three that afternoon, I put my saddle back on Apache and went along.

We dropped our horses off at a livery and walked up the street. Just short of the mercantile, Charlie pulled up short and ran his hand across his mouth. "Reckon this'll be our last day in a real town for a good spell," he said. "How about one last drink?"

"Never cared much for the stuff," I said, "but I'll keep you company while you have one."

"Fair enough. Let's go."

Going into the nearest saloon, Charlie went to the bar and came away holding a shot of whiskey and a beer chaser. We found a table and sat down. Charlie downed the whiskey, shivered, took a long pull on the beer.

"I don't drink often myself," he said, "but a shot of whiskey and a beer is kind of a tradition up here. They say a man who leaves without drinking both won't come back in the spring."

"Do you believe that?"

Charlie took another drink of beer. "Won't say I do, and won't say I don't. But why take chances?"

As we sat there, a young man came through the door. The pack on his back must have weighed a hundred and fifty pounds or better, but he carried it with ease. Our table wasn't far from the door, and his eyes met mine. "Would you mind keeping your eye on my pack for a minute, mister?" he asked. "I'd like to get myself a beer, and maybe a plate of food, if they have anything worth eating."

"Set it down," I said. "I'll keep an eye on it."

He slipped the pack off. "Thank you," he said.

He went to the bar and came back a minute later, holding a beer. "They say the food will take a bit."

"Join us, if you'd like," I said. "Might as well wait together."

He sat down, sipped the beer, stretched his back. "Never figured on carrying weight like that when I started for Alaska," he said. "I thought dogs and mules did all the hard work."

"Dogs, mules, and men," Charlie said. "You going over the Chilkoot?"

"No, sir. I have a mule load of supplies besides that pack, so I'm going by way of White Pass. They say you can't get a mule over the Chilkoot."

"Getting one through White Pass is hard enough," Charlie said. "How many in your party?"

"Just me. Why?"

"You ever traveled wild country before?"

"No, sir. I was raised in Chicago."

"Traveling alone is dangerous, even for a man with experience, but for a man who doesn't know what to expect, it can kill you quick. My advice is to team up with a few men. It'll make your trip safer."

"You can go along with us," I said, "if you don't mind going slow. Might take us a month or more to get through, but we'll get there."

"I can't wait," he said. "I've heard the best claims are being grabbed fast. Every day I wait means less chance of finding gold."

"Better late and alive than early and dead," Charlie said. "Going alone means you might not make it."

"I'll make it," he said. "I have to make it. I have three kids back in Chicago, and their mother died a year ago. I want them to have a better life, and a better education than I ever had. This is the only way I know how to make it happen. I *have* to make it through."

We talked until his food came. He ate quickly, then stood up and shouldered his pack. "My name is Martin Springer," he said. "Look me up when you get to Dawson and I'll buy you a drink."

He walked out, tall, young, and proud. When he was gone I looked at Charlie. "Do you think he'll make it through White Pass alone?"

"Odds are he'll make it," Charlie said, "but he's taking a big chance."

CHAPTER 12

NEXT MORNING WE ate breakfast early, then sat drinking coffee, waiting for the sun to warm things up a little. At ten minutes past nine I stood up and tossed the last of my coffee on the fire. "We might as well get started," I said. "Dead Horse Trail is waiting."

"I just hope this drive don't cause folks to rename it Dead Cow Trail," Charlie said.

"Getting jittery?" Billy asked.

"You're danged right," Charlie said. "You ain't seen that pass, boy, or you'd be nervous, too."

We started off slow, keeping the cattle pointed where we wanted them to go, but letting them set their own pace in getting there. A thousand or more men were going over the trail, and at almost any time you could see men walking along ahead or behind.

Charlie said the Chilkoot was even worse, that men were often lined up nose to neck all the way from the base to the summit and down the other side. All the men, mules, and horses on the trail kind of jammed things up a bit, especially since cattle don't give a damn who has the right of way.

Still, other than the occasional cow that bolted from the herd, only to get mired down in mud or snow, the cattle had a surprisingly easy time of it. Then we came to Dead Horse Trail. When we were close enough, we found a place to let the herd mill around, and took some time to decide how best to start.

Charlie said, "It'll take forever to take 'em through a few at a time, but I don't see no other way."

99

"All right," I said. "Billy, let's you and me cut out ten head and start them through."

We cut out the first ten head fool enough to let us get close, and we started them up the trail. They didn't want to go, and I didn't blame them. There was more than one place where a cow, or a man, could fall far enough to grow old before he hit bottom.

When we reached the first real piece of thread trail, I risked a glance at Billy. His face was twisted into a pale mask. He saw me looking at him and opened his mouth to say something, then closed it without a word. I knew exactly how he felt.

We made it almost halfway through the bad stretch before anything happened. A big steer two back from the leader put his hoof down on a piece of loose rock. The rock slid, and the steer went down, tried to get up, and fell right off the trail. It made a sickening thump hitting a boulder forty feet below.

That was the only cow we lost, but by the time we left that eleven-mile stretch behind us and found a place to let the cattle graze, it was well after dark. There was no way of getting back until the next day, so we built a fire and chewed on old biscuits from Billy's saddlebags.

Leaving Billy with the nine cows, I left at dawn the next morning and rode back to Charlie and Paul. They were eating lunch when I arrived. " 'Bout time you made it back," Charlie said. "How'd it go?"

"We lost one steer," I said. "Could've been worse."

Sitting down near the fire, I ate lunch as I talked. "We did learn one thing," I said. "More than one man per group of cows is wasted. There's no place for the cattle to go, and one man can push them through."

"Do you think we can risk taking more than ten at a time?" Paul asked.

"Be a risk," I said, "but we might try a few more. Trouble is, we can't get another group through today because it is too late. Much as I hate to do it, I think we'll have to leave Billy where he is for another night.

"I'll start another bunch of cattle through at dawn. Paul, you can follow with a second group two hours later. If both groups get through, you and Billy can ride back, spend the night here, and start two more groups the next morning, while I spend the night over there."

"You sure we can't take them through all at once?" Charlie asked. "This way is going to waste an awful lot of time."

"They're your cattle," I said, "but I don't think there's a chance of getting more than fifteen or so through in one group unless you want to lose a lot of beef. Later in the summer we might pull it off, depending on how dry the trail gets, but not now."

Charlie nodded. "I expected as much, but I had to ask. When do I take a bunch through?"

"Sure you're up to it?"

"Boy, didn't we chase these cattle together last winter, and that in the middle of a blizzard? This can't be any worse."

I smiled. "This is bad enough, but I've never been as cold as I was last winter. Let's see, tomorrow Paul and I'll take groups through. Day after that will be wasted, because Paul and Billy will have to ride back here. The next day you can take the first bunch through. How's that?"

"Fine. But it appears to me that we'll be wasting one day in every two doing it this way. Suppose we hire a couple of fellows, one to stay with the cattle at each end of the trail? That way we can take two bunches a day through. Me an' Paul will have two going through while you and Billy are riding back this way. Day after that you two will be driving and we'll be riding back. Should cut our time in half."

"Makes sense," I said. "There's plenty of men passing along the trail who'd like to put a few extra dollars in their pockets."

There were, as it turned out, more than a few men along the trail who'd spent their last dollar buying supplies back in Skagway. Lunch wasn't much more than over before we'd hired a couple of brothers named Jake and Samuel Strunk. They'd come to Alaska from Arkansas. Jake was seventeen and Samuel was just ten months older. "They's nine boys and four girls in the family," Jake told us. "And our cabin didn't have but three rooms. That was bad enough, but then our oldest sister got herself hitched and had twins.

"They all moved into the cabin with us, and it got so a body couldn't take a step without his foot coming down on a young'un. Then a circuit-ridin' preacher came by for supper, and he had himself a real newspaper in his saddlebags.

"Well, sir, he took to reading it out loud after eatin', and when he got to a story about all the gold they been findin' up here, why, me an' Sam just plain got a case of get-goin' fever."

"That's sure enough a fact," Sam put in. "We didn't have no money, so we taken our time an' worked our way north. And here we are, ready to get rich."

"I guess your folks would like that," Charlie said. "Be nice if you could help them out, maybe build them a bigger house."

"That'd be great," Jake said, "but I think we already made them happy just by leaving. That's two less in the cabin."

"For a time," Sam said. "I reckon Ma or the girls will make up for it after a time."

They were quite a pair, and I liked them right off. In truth, they reminded me of the backwoods folks I grew up with. The only difference between them and me was that my mother had a sister who was a schoolmarm, so Ma made every one of us go to school. She made sure we read books and the like when we were home. Pa claimed not to see the sense in it, but by the time I was old enough to leave home, Ma had him reading almost as much as the rest of us.

"How does two dollars a day sound?" I asked.

They looked at each other. "Mister," Jake said. "Ain't neither of us ever made that kind of money."

"It's settled then. There isn't time to take more cattle through today, but if one of you is up to it, I'd like you to take some food on to our friend, and tell him to start back as soon as it's light."

"I'll do 'er," Sam said. "I can walk that far on my hands."

Leaving most of his supplies at our camp, he loaded up with food and started walking. He had a light step and sure feet, even over the rough trail. I figured he'd reach Billy in five hours or less.

Come morning I started fifteen head of cattle over the trail, but I hadn't gone more than a few hundred yards when I realized more than ten was a serious mistake. In fact, we'd probably lose fewer cows if we cut even that number in half. Compromising, I cut all but eight head out and drove them back to camp. "Eight at a time," I told Paul and Charlie. "Any more than that and we'll lose one or two every trip."

They nodded and I took off back to the eight steers I'd left on the trail. Not that they were going to get lost without me. The one nice thing about that rough section of trail was that it didn't give cattle, horses, or men much in the way of choices. You went straight ahead or straight back. All we had to do was keep the cattle walking, not let them turn back, and sooner or later we'd get to the other side of the trail.

On the first trip through we'd lost a steer, but this time I made it with all eight. Billy made much better time coming back without cattle, of course, and we met up when I was no more than a quarter of the way through. It wasn't ideal country to sit and chat, so we did little more than nod in passing.

The cattle went over the trail quite a bit slower than a man walking, but occasionally the bunch would catch up with fellows sitting down and taking a rest. It was hard not to smile when they looked up and saw a thousand-pound steer coming down the trail toward them. They didn't know whether to sit quiet and let it pass, jump for cover, or take off running. They needn't have worried. A cow might not be the brightest animal God ever created, but it's smarter than most give it credit for, and even the dumbest steer we had knew better than to start running after someone on that narrow, treacherous trail.

Coming through Dead Horse Trail, I ran my eight head of cattle in with the nine from the first trip, then started fixing supper. I'm not much of a hand when it comes to cooking, so I made do by putting on coffee, a pot of beans, and a pan of salt pork. I dearly loved the sourdough bread that Charlie was always baking in the Dutch oven, but oven and sourdough starter were both on the other side of the trail.

Besides, I didn't think I could make a passable bread even if I had the stuff. Before the drive was over, I thought, I'd have to make Charlie teach me how to do it.

Sam didn't seem to mind my cooking, though. Leastways, he put away his share and seemed to enjoy doing it.

After eating, we both leaned back with a cup of coffee and just took in the country. "I thought we saw somethin' when we hit the Rocky Mountains," he said. "Then the Sierras near took my breath. But you know what? I think this country's got 'em both beat all hollow."

Mountains rose up all around us, and in the distance we could see a whole range fading off to nothing. "I won't argue that point," I said. "This is a big, wild country. I've never seen anything like it."

Two hours later, with dark pushing in around us, Paul

brought in seven steers. "Lost one," he said. "It was walking along fine, and the next second it was gone. I still don't know what happened."

Come morning, we started back over the trail, meeting Billy driving a bunch, then Charlie following along an hour behind.

On his trip, Charlie saw a man's hand protruding from a pile of snow and rock fifty feet below the trail. He found a way down and dug the body out. It was Martin Springer. I went back with him later and helped free the body. We buried him as best we could and put up a crude marker.

On the way back to our fire, Charlie was silent for a long time. When he at last turned to me and spoke, his face seemed older. "I warned him about going it alone. Why didn't he listen?"

"He was too young and in too much of a hurry, I guess. You did all you could."

"Maybe. But what about his kids? Their mother dead, and now their father. It bothers me."

"Me, too, Charlie. But what can we do? There wasn't a thing on him with an address, so we can't even write to tell them what happened."

"I know. . . ."

Neither of us said another word all the way to the camp. Men die. We both knew that. But sometimes they die for no good reason. Martin Springer had been impatient, even foolhardy, but it was plain bad luck that killed him.

We had a snow, and lost a day because of it. Then a hard rain melted most of the snow, but turned sections of the trail into bog. We waited three days for things to dry up enough to start driving more cattle. There were other delays, and all told, it took us twelve days to get the last cow safely through Dead Horse Trail. We lost nine head in the process.

"I don't like it," Charlie said. "We figured three days to get the cattle through, and it took twelve. If we can't figure better'n that, well, I don't like the idea of spending the winter inside Alaska, but it might shape up that way."

"It should get easier once we're all the way through White Pass," I said. "It's only May. We have time to spare."

"It's June," Charlie said. "I been keeping track. And in Alaska you never have time to spare. It gets mighty hot up here in the summer, but she doesn't last too long at all.

"The worst of the winter comes late this far west and north, but it can snow just about any month of the year, and it doesn't take much to shut down these passes."

"I kind of like it up here," Billy said. "I've been thinkin' about staying after the drive is over. Might stake myself a claim and look for gold."

"You ain't seen an Alaskan winter yet," Charlie said. "Near every cheechako up here takes one look around and decides he's gonna stay. Then winter comes along, the thermometer hits forty or fifty below and holds there for weeks on end. You get cooped up in a ten-foot-square cabin with three other men for a few months when it's that cold, and like as not you'll forget all about staying."

"Maybe," Billy said, "but I aim to give it a try."

We pushed the cattle as hard as we dared, and the day arrived when we came out of White Pass. The land was less treacherous and reminded me, in fact, a bit of Montana. But it didn't take long for other trouble to come along. Jake and Samuel Strunk had left us once the cattle were through Dead Horse Trail, so we were down to four men again, and that meant we were always spread out a bit when driving the cattle.

We were pushing the cattle along the base of a spruce-covered knoll. Billy was riding point, Paul had the right flank, I had the left, and Charlie was riding drag. Paul was closest to the knoll, and all at once his horse whinnied and tried to dance away. Next thing you know there's a bear charging out of the trees right at him.

We had the cattle strung out a bit, so I was no more than thirty yards from Paul, and when I saw the bear I yanked out my rifle and jacked a cartridge into the chamber. Paul was fighting his horse with one hand, and trying to get his rifle free with the other.

I didn't know what the bear was after, likely one of the cows, but in getting to them it went right through Paul. One swipe of a massive paw knocked Paul's horse off its feet. Keeping his grip on the rifle, Paul rolled free and came up to one knee.

The bear was going after a cow, and the whole herd stampeded. Paul brought the rifle to his shoulder and fired. The bear roared, wheeled around toward Paul and charged, looking like a runaway locomotive. It was big. Godalmighty big!

Paul was firing as fast as he could, and I joined in, levering shot after shot into the charging bear. My rifle clicked empty, and Paul disappeared under the bear. Dropping the rifle, I pulled my Colt and stuck spurs into Apache's sides. Only when we reached the bear did I realize it wasn't moving.

All I could see of Paul was one foot and the barrel of his rifle. Part of his face must have been free, though, because I could hear his voice.

"Get this danged thing off of me. It must weigh a ton."

Billy had been too far up front to get in a shot, and Charlie had been too far behind, but they came riding up. We had to rope the bear and roll it off Paul with a horse. He came to his feet cursing, gasping for air, and covered with the bear's blood, but unharmed except for a knot on the back of his head.

The cattle were another story. They were scattered to hell and gone. Rounding them up might take days.

"We'd best hustle," Charlie said. "You can bet that isn't the only bear in these parts, and they all love beef. There's wolves about, too. Yes, sir, we'd best get those cattle back together fast."

We started right then, riding our horses hard. By the end of the day we had sixty-three of the cattle back together. That left almost half out there on their own. Some wouldn't make it through the night.

CHAPTER 13

WHEN IT WAS too dark to hunt cattle, we built a fire and collapsed around it. Charlie sat for a spell, then took a torch-sized piece of wood and wrapped one end with a piece of heavy cloth torn from a raggedy set of longjohns. He dug a can of kerosene from the supplies, doused the cloth around the stick, and touched it to the fire.

Then he walked off into the darkness. "Where you going?" Billy asked.

"It just isn't in me to waste meat," Charlie said. "I'm going over to skin that bear they shot."

"Tonight?"

"Meat'll be spoiled by morning. Won't take long."

"Hang on," I said. "I'll go along with you. Never saw a bear skinned before, let alone one that big."

"Come to think on it," Billy said, "neither have I. Guess I'll go along, too."

"Not me," Paul said. "I never saw a bear that big, but I've skinned a couple smaller ones. Besides, I seen all of that bear I want to."

Because of the need to start rounding up the scattered herd, we'd made camp less than two hundred yards from the dead bear. When the huge shape came into the torch-light, we saw three wolves moving in on the carcass.

Charlie carried a pistol, an old Army Colt converted to take cartridges, but he didn't like wearing a holster, so most of the time he carried it in his belt. Now he pulled the pistol and fired twice. The first bullet kicked dirt right between the front paws of a wolf, and the second bullet cut hair from its tail.

The wolves darted away into the night. "Wolves up here ain't like the ones back home," Charlie said. "They'll back off when they have to, but they ain't afraid of nothing. Not even a man."

We gathered wood and built a good-sized fire for added light and warmth, then Charlie went to work on the bear. Moving the massive beast around so Charlie could get his knife where he wanted it was the tough part, but once he gutted the bear it was easier.

Charlie handled his knife as well as any buffalo skinner, and with our muscle to help shift the bear around the way he wanted it, the animal was skinned in nothing flat. The body of the bear was gray in the firelight, and without the hide and fur, it looked remarkably like a man.

After slicing fifty pounds of the best meat off the body, Charlie went to work on the hide. He spent forty-five minutes scraping away fat and clinging bits of meat, then rolled the hide into a tight ball. "Still got a lot of work to do on it," he said, "but that's enough for tonight."

"What're you going to do with it?" Billy asked.

"Danged if I know," Charlie said. "A hide like that comes in real handy during winter, but we don't hardly have room on a mule to carry it. Just hate to see useful things go to waste. I'll find something to do with it."

Charlie counted eleven bullet holes in the hide, but the one that stopped the bear had gone through its eye. "That one yours or Paul's?" Billy asked.

"I was aiming for the chest," I said. "I expect Paul was, too. One of us got lucky."

"If you hadn't, Paul wouldn't be with us," Charlie said. "A thirty-thirty is too light for bear."

Off in the night a wolf howled, long and forlorn. A second wolf answered, then a third.

"Lucky there's no moon," Charlie said. "Our cattle should be all right until morning, but then the wolves will start hunting them."

Another wolf howled. It was a longer, deeper, more drawn-out sound than the others. "That's an old lobo wolf," Charlie said. "He runs alone, fights alone, and kills alone. You run into that fellow, put a bullet in him fast."

The rolled bear hide weighed a hundred pounds or more, and I carried it back to camp for Charlie. I was panting some before we got back to Paul. Dropping the hide, I flopped down beside it and reached for the coffee-pot.

"I ain't sure," Paul said, "but I think we got company not too far off."

"What makes you say that?" Billy asked.

"You can't see it from here," Paul said, "but walk over near the horses and look straight east and up just a touch."

Billy walked the thirty yards to the horses, stood for two minutes looking east, then walked back over to the fire. "Looks like a campfire," he said. "It's a good piece off, though."

"Not as far as you'd think," Paul said. "I think it's a small fire."

"Maybe we ought to ride over and see who it is," Charlie said.

I thought about it. "No, not all of us. Two or three should stay with the cattle. Just you and me, Charlie. Let's go see who's out there."

We saddled our horses and rode away from camp. Charlie knew the country better than I did, so he led the way. The fire was a small one, but still almost a half mile away. It had been built in the middle of a tiny clearing almost completely surrounded by thick spruce trees. It was pure luck that we had seen it at all.

We weren't more than forty yards from the fire when we got our first real look at the men sitting around it. Charlie pulled his horse up short. "Talk quiet," he said. "That's an Indian camp."

That stopped me. "Are they friendly?"

"No tellin'. I think they're Kutchin . . . maybe Koyukon. Either way, they're unpredictable at times."

"Ever known anybody, white or red, who wasn't?"

"Nope. Not when you put it that way."

"Want to ride away?"

For a full thirty seconds Charlie didn't answer. "I was about to say yes, but look close at what they're eating."

"Meat," I said. "So?"

"Beef," Charlie said. "Look under that big spruce to the right of the fire."

I looked. A haunch of meat hung from a limb. It still had the hide on, and it was plainly the hide of a cow.

"Probably saw it running wild and shot it," I said. "Can't really blame them."

"I don't," Charlie said. "But it gives me an idea. I know a bit about this country, but not a speck compared to them. Like as not, they could find every stray we have without workin' up a sweat."

"Do you think they would?"

"Not but one way to find out. Let's go ask 'em."

"All right, but keep your eyes open. I only see two men, but there may be more."

Charlie let out a yell so the Indians would know we were coming. They never twitched. We rode up, stopping forty feet from the fire. Charlie said something in a language I didn't know. After a minute one of the Indians said something in return.

"He says we can join him at the fire."

We sat down and Charlie started talking, using his hands as much as his mouth. It went back and forth between them, and I sat listening, but not knowing what they were saying. At last Charlie took out his pipe and filled it as he spoke to me.

"Didn't take them long to learn from the white man," he said. "They're willing to help find our strays, but they want to know what we'll pay. I offered a dollar a head, they want two dollars."

"Pay it," I said. "Those cattle are worth close to a thousand dollars a head in Dawson."

"Isn't that," Charlie said. "A dollar a head is fair pay for the work involved, and they know it. They're making too much of a fuss over how hard it'll be to find 'em. I think they already know where most of the cattle are."

"Maybe, but we don't."

"You got a point," Charlie said. "All right, two dollars a head it is. But I don't like it."

I kept my eyes on the Indian who'd done most of the talking. He wasn't a young man, and when Charlie spoke again, the Indian's face didn't change, but the twinkle in his eye did. "He says they will start hunting when the sun comes up," Charlie said. "Thinks he got the better of me, too."

"We'll know tomorrow," I said.

We shook hands all around, then climbed on our horses and started back to our own camp. Fifty yards from the Indians' fire I turned and looked back. Where two Indians had been sitting around the fire, there were now four. "They don't take chances," I said.

"That's one of the things I like about 'em," Charlie said. "Anybody takes a chance in this country is asking for a quick funeral."

We took turns riding guard on the cattle all night long, keeping them tightly bunched and hoping another bear or a pack of wolves didn't want beef for a midnight snack. Several times it sounded like the wolves were moving closer, but each time they retreated into the night.

The mosquitoes hadn't been too bad up to that point, but now they almost drove us crazy. The only way to sleep was to cover our heads and leave only the tiniest opening for air; riding guard on the cattle was pure torture. None of us slept much except for Charlie. When morning came Paul asked what his secret was. Charlie grinned.

"Bear grease," he said. "The skeeters don't like it. Rub it on any skin not covered, and they'll pretty much leave you alone."

"Pass it around," Billy said. "Those things like to drove me crazy last night."

Charlie went to the stack of supplies and came out with a large tobacco tin. He pulled the lid off and handed it to Billy. Billy sniffed the contents, coughed, jerked his face away. "Peeyew," he said. "That stuff stinks to high heaven."

"It's that or the skeeters," Charlie said. "Take your choice."

Billy handed the tin back to Charlie. "Reckon I'll take the skeeters," he said.

"Suit yourself."

After breakfast, we saddled up and started to hunt for strays, leaving John to watch the herd. We rode a hundred yards apart, hoping to cut the track of a steer. We'd been out maybe half an hour when Billy suddenly spurred his horse and rode over to me.

"You ain't going to believe what's coming over yonder," he said. "Those Indians you all talked to last night must be part-time cowboys. They're coming along through the trees pushing twenty-five or thirty head of cattle, and they're doin' it on foot."

"Ride over and tell Charlie," I said. "I'll go meet them."

Billy stuck spurs to his horse and took off in the direction I'd last seen Charlie, and I trotted over to meet the Indians. I saw the cattle first, and tried to get a count. Twenty-three was the number I got. Then four more head moved out where I could see them.

Driving cattle on foot is tricky and dangerous. Range cattle are at best half wild, and at worst they'd sooner gore a man than eat. The Indians seemed to know this, and they were keeping their distance, getting the cattle to go where they wanted by standing where they didn't want them. In shying away from the distant men, the cattle were heading for our camp.

As I sat there waiting for the cattle to pass and the Indians to move closer, Billy and Charlie came riding up.

"How you reckon they did it?" Billy asked. "How do you suppose they rounded up all those cattle overnight?"

"Rounded up, hell," Charlie said. "Those cattle must have run themselves out and stayed close together. And those danged Indians knew just where they were when we talked to 'em last night."

"Looks like we'll come up six or seven head short," I said, "but it's hard to complain. I didn't think we'd get this many back together."

"I'll bet a dollar against a worn dime those Indians know where the others are, too," Charlie said. "Likely they kept 'em back for food."

"Easier than hunting," I said. "Well, let's go see what they have to say for themselves."

As we rode up, the Indian who had done most of the talking at their camp moved up to Charlie. They went back and forth for a few minutes, and at last Charlie took out his money and counted out fifty-four dollars. The Indian took it without a word.

The moment the money changed hands, the Indians simply turned around and vanished into the woods. We pushed the cattle back to the main herd, and after packing the camp, we started down the trail.

We weren't actually in Alaska—we had left Alaska and crossed into the Yukon right outside of Skagway. To most of the gold seekers, however, there was no difference between Alaska and the Yukon. They followed the gold strikes, wandering back and forth over the line without thought or care.

It made me wonder if there wasn't an easier way to get cattle up here, maybe by driving them over from Canada.

"Lots of folks wonder about that," Charlie said. "If you think the way we came was hard, just try coming in by land. There's breaks and choked passes a man on foot can't fight his way through, much less a loaded pack mule or a hundred head of cantankerous cattle.

"Reckon it won't be too many years before somebody cuts a way through there, but I'll be sorry to see it. Right now a man has to work at it just to get into this country. That keeps the weaklings and the cowards out, if it don't do nothing else."

In a way, I understood Charlie's point. He wasn't the only one who felt that way, and rough as the men were who flocked to the goldfields, no one could deny they were strong and brave.

Even the women who came, and there were plenty, had a full measure of strength and courage. Some even came alone and went into business for themselves. There were prostitutes, of course, but most of the women were good, decent people. They opened laundries or bakeries, and some few even staked claims and worked the placer gold alongside the men.

That evening we met such a woman. As was most often the case, Charlie was coming along at the rear, keeping the cattle moving and trailing the pack mules along behind him, and Billy was up front riding point. Billy was having trouble with a bull that kept trying to break from the herd. The bull broke for cover several times, but each time Billy cut it off and drove it back to the rest.

Then the bull got smart and waited until Billy was chasing a steer before making his try. This time it reached thick cover, with Billy tearing along behind.

The bull ran right through a campsite, and so did Billy. The camp was in an out-of-the-way spot next to a small stream, and the woman whose camp it was must have felt in need of a bath, because when Billy rode through she was sitting in the water, wearing only what God gave her.

Finding a naked woman taking a bath was the last thing in the world Billy expected in the brush a hundred miles from nowhere, and he was understandably surprised. So surprised that he forgot to watch where he was going. His horse passed under a low limb, but Billy still had his eyes on the stream and didn't see it.

The limb caught him on the forehead and took him right out of the saddle. The woman hastened to get dressed, then went to see if he was still alive. He was, though he had a wicked knot on his head, and it was an hour before he knew which end was up. The woman heard our cattle and ran out to where we could see her. She told us what happened and I rode over to check on Billy.

He was sitting up, but like I said, he kind of babbled for a time, with no idea what had happened. We made camp close by, and while Billy recuperated, we got to know the woman.

CHAPTER 14

HER NAME WAS Hannie Welch, and at first glance no one would ever take her for the kind of woman who'd be out there alone in the middle of the wilderness. Her hair was long, sandy brown, and pulled back in a ponytail. Her eyes were deep brown, her lips full, her face dark and pretty.

Hannie stood almost six feet tall, however, and weighed something like one-fifty. Her hands were calloused, hard as any man's, and she was obviously a woman who'd known brutal work most of her life. She wore jeans, boots, a flannel shirt, and a leather jacket. She had no pistol that I could see, but she kept a rifle close and handled it with easy familiarity.

All of us were curious about her, but it was Paul who got Hannie to talking about herself. "Ma'am," he said, "I reckon it's none of my business, but I'd sure be curious to know how you came to be out here."

Hannie shrugged. "A woman has to make a living just like a man. I've two children waiting for me back in Missouri, and if they're to have a better life, I'm the one who has to earn the money."

"I'd think a woman like you would have a husband to do for her," Billy said. "I mean, you're an attractive woman, Miss Welch."

She looked Billy right in the eye. "Mister," she said, "I had a husband. He swore he loved me, then stayed just long enough to get me pregnant with twins. When he left he took the last bit of money we had. A woman with two kids and no husband is hard against the wall. There just ain't many jobs for a decent woman. Not that pay enough to raise kids on."

"How did you get from Missouri all the way up here?" I asked. "That isn't a cheap trip."

"I worked every job around home I could find. After two years I had enough saved to get here, so I left my twins with my sister and came. When I reached Skagway I was broke, but I met a lady who loaned me a grubstake for supplies, so here I am."

"I admire that, ma'am," Charlie said. "I surely do. But you're going about it the hard way. Not one man in five hundred travels to Dawson City overland. Best way is to go by water, even if you have to build your own boat.

"This country is full of bogs and surrounded by mountains. She's filled with Indians, wild animals, white men who'd love to find a woman alone, and weather that can kill you quick. If it wasn't for these cows, I'd never think of trying for Dawson by land."

"Traveling by water might be easier," Hannie said, "but it ain't for me. I talked to folks about it in Skagway, and I didn't like what I heard.

"They tell me some men wait months for the ice to break up, then either spend more weeks building a boat, or hurry things up by buildin' one that'll sink before they get a mile. A lot of people get to Dawson by boat, but from what I hear, a lot get drowned on the way.

"Besides, there won't be a good claim left in Dawson by the time I get there. I plan on panning the small streams as I go. Who knows, maybe I can start a gold rush all my own."

Hannie ate supper with us, then went back to her own camp. But I think she was on all our minds as we went to sleep. We pulled out at daylight, and Hannie was there to see us off.

The far northern land is a beautiful place, and no two ways about it. Summer was full upon us and the land had come alive under the influence. We crossed a meadow nearly a quarter mile long and equally wide, and every square inch of it was filled with wild mountain flowers of a dozen varieties and shades.

Birds and animals were everywhere. Geese and duck flew over us by the thousands, moose fed in the lakes, and bears fed off fish and any animal they could bring down. Twice we even came across grizzlies standing in waist-high grass, eating it as happily as any cow.

Traveling across that land, it was hard to believe anyone would pay a dollar a pound for beef. We had fresh meat every day, and we had our choice of the kind. But I knew what Charlie had said was true. In Dawson it would be different.

In Skagway I heard a man say that the whole damn north was either too high and covered by snow, or too low and filled with water. He wasn't far wrong, and getting the herd to Dawson couldn't be done by pointing a straight line and following it. We spent a good deal of our time scouting miles ahead, not wanting to steer ourselves into a bad section of country that we couldn't cross with cattle.

There were lakes to get around, rivers to cross, and too many places where we'd risk losing cattle trying to get through. In short, we were making poor time, and none of us knew how to speed things up.

I'd been on cattle drives in Texas, and down there a man could easily drive cattle twenty miles in a day, though many a rancher wouldn't do that, preferring to cut the distance in half and let the cattle fatten as they walked.

As the crow flies, we had something over four hundred miles to go, but neither we nor the cattle had any wings that I could find. So we would have to travel close to six hundred miles to reach Dawson, and we probably weren't going to make ten miles a day, much less twenty. The country was simply too rough, too unpredictable, too unknown.

It was a land of gold dust and sled dogs, of men looking not for a way to get cattle through, but for a way to quickly reach the latest gold strike by foot or boat or dogsled. Even those who knew the country well couldn't be relied on when asked about a good route for cattle, because they had never looked at the country through a cowboy's eyes.

They were city men, country men, and foreign men. They came from all parts of the world and from all walks of life, but they all had one thing in common—gold. Gold filled their thoughts in the day and their dreams in the night. Any one of them would pay handsomely for a thick steak cooked to a turn and laid out on their plate . . . but not one gave a damn how the beef made it from Skagway to Dawson.

So we pushed on, spending half our time scouting, and half driving cattle. Some days we made twelve miles, other days we made two.

August came and we were still in the heart of the wilderness, hundreds of miles from Dawson.

"We ain't goin' to make it," Charlie said. "We ain't goin' to reach Dawson and still get out before winter."

I didn't like it, but I was afraid Charlie was right. Summer gets hot in that part of the north. Temperatures close to a hundred aren't uncommon, in fact. But summer doesn't stay around to wear out its welcome. As one sourdough put it, "Spring lasts three days, summer lasts three weeks, and if autumn ever visited the Yukon, it came after midnight and left before dawn."

The thought of staying for the winter appealed to Billy, and he'd talked Paul into staying with him after the drive ended. But Charlie wanted out to pay off the mortgage on his ranch and send his daughter some money, and I wanted out because of Angie.

Yet did it matter whether I stayed or left? So long as Fergus Thornton had a price on my head, Angie and I could never be together. We had Taminy Kisling working to make Fergus back down, but it might mean nothing. Taminy struck me as a smart, capable man with no backup in him, but Fergus Thornton was still the old bull of the woods, and he wouldn't backwater for any man.

But the only way to know was to go see, though I expected Angie would send a letter to Skagway if she had any news.

In short, I wanted out before winter, and so did Charlie, so we put in longer hours scouting and driving. We hit a good stretch and made a hundred miles in nine days because Charlie was an old hand at finding his way through rough country, and it began to look as if we stood a chance.

But in our haste to reach Dawson we took our minds off the dangers around us, and we paid a hard price.

If Charlie's calculations were right, the herd was walking along a tributary of Beaver Creek, and we had a little less than two hundred miles to go. That was still a long way, but with luck we'd reach Dawson in less than a month, sell the cattle, and hustle back by boat before winter closed the mountain passes.

Charlie killed a moose that evening, and we made an early camp to give him time to cut out enough meat to last a few days.

"You haven't eaten until you've had moose nose," Charlie said. "Just you wait."

We were skeptical, but Charlie cut out the meat and served it at supper. Our first bites were cautious, but after we had a taste the only sound was forks striking tin plates as we dug for more.

Our camp was seventy yards from the cattle, but somebody rode guard at all times, and we switched off during the night. The way it worked out that night, I started the watch and Paul would finish with the last ride of the night. My hours in the saddle passed without anything more exciting happening than some kind of night bird, likely an owl, swooping down and knocking my hat off.

I rode back to camp when my shift was over, woke Billy for his turn, crawled into my blankets, and went to sleep.

When I opened my eyes it was light enough to see, but not so late that I couldn't have slept another half hour without feeling guilty. But Charlie was already awake, sitting on his blankets, yawning and stretching. When he stood up and tossed a few sticks on the fire to get it going again, I sighed and rose up.

"Rise and shine," Charlie said. "Man won't get nowhere in life if he spends his whole morning in bed."

I told Charlie what he could do with his opinions, pulled my boots on, and walked down to the stream. The water on my face and hands brought me fully awake, and after taking care of my morning chores, I went back to camp.

Charlie had coffee on, but it wasn't ready yet, so I sat down and rolled a smoke. I had enough tobacco left for two or three more days, and that was it. I wasn't looking forward to doing without.

The noise Charlie made putting breakfast on woke Billy up. "When we get to Dawson," he said, "I'm going to rent myself a real bed and sleep for a week."

Billy went down to the stream, came back, and sat down. The coffee was ready, and we each poured a cup. Billy looked out toward the herd. "Paul should've come in by now," he said. "He ain't one to miss breakfast."

"He'll be in before long," I said.

"Probably sleepin' under a tree," Charlie said. "He'll be along when he wakes up."

Fifteen minutes passed, and there was still no sign of Paul. The herd was set so we could see a part of it from camp, but I watched for all of that fifteen minutes without seeing Paul make a round. I went over and saddled Apache.

"I don't like it," I said. "I'm going to ride down and see what's keeping him."

As I stepped into the saddle and started Apache toward the herd, an eagle screamed, and I glanced at it. When I looked back toward the herd, a movement caught my eye. It came from the trees at the far side of the herd, and it was nothing more than a flicker of brown through the green of the trees.

Paul was nowhere to be seen. I didn't like it. The eagle screaming was the only sound to be heard. Not a bird or an animal made a sound. Slipping the thong off my Colt, I walked Apache toward the spot where I'd seen the movement.

From less than thirty yards I saw motion again, and I realized it was a riderless horse. Maybe Charlie was right. Maybe Paul had let the long night get to him. Maybe he'd sat down under a tree to rest a bit and fallen asleep. Walking Apache closer, I saw Paul on the ground close to the horse. My heart stopped as I realized he was facedown, and two arrows were sticking in the center of his back.

Something moved in the corner of my vision, and I turned to look. A man was standing there, but it wasn't a bow he held, it was a rifle, and it was pointed right at me.

My reflexes took over and my hand snapped the Colt from the holster, thumbing the hammer back as it came into line with the man. He fired first. Red flame burst from the muzzle of the rifle, and something seemed to explode inside my head. Thought left my mind, but I dimly felt my own Colt jump as I pulled the trigger.

Everything went red, then black. My next conscious thought was that somehow I was still in the saddle, but Apache was running hard under me. Through the haze I heard a hammering of shots.

Have to get back, I thought. They'll need help. Got to get back.

The reins weren't in my hand. I was holding on by

clinging to the saddlehorn, and doing that poorly. One foot was out of the stirrup, and I tried desperately to get it back in. A wave of dizziness passed over me, and I almost blacked out. My thoughts were of staying in the saddle. If I could stay in the saddle, Apache would somehow get me back to camp.

I felt Apache slow to a trot, then to a walk. Somehow, I sat up in the saddle. Everything was hazy, spinning wildly, and my thoughts wouldn't sort themselves out. Stay in the saddle, I thought. Stay in the saddle.

Then everything went black and I felt myself falling. Without knowing where I was going, or why I wanted to go there, I started crawling. Then I passed out again. For a long time I knew nothing at all.

CHAPTER 15

THOUGHTS RETURNED TO my mind, but for a long time they existed in darkness. Where was I? What had happened to me? Why was it so dark and cold? Memories of gunshots and pain forced their way through the darkness, and it all came flooding back.

Awareness came slowly to the pitch-black world of my mind. My eyes were closed, the lids opening slowly at my command. Opening them helped only a little. My face was in the needle-carpeted dirt, and it took some time to realize the white blob inches from my face was my own hand.

I moved, and with the movement came pain. It split my head like a lightning bolt. I groaned, gave up the effort. In time I tried again, and this time managed to roll over. Using my feet more than my hands, I pushed myself backward toward the trunk of a tree, then up to a sitting position against it.

Breathing hard, eyes closed tight against the throbbing pain, I reached fingers upward and explored my head, afraid of what I would find.

There was a long, deep gash on the left side of my forehead. It was as wide as my finger was thick, and at least three inches long. It seemed to go all the way to the bone. My hand came away bloody.

Sitting there, I took stock of my situation. It was nearly dark by the look of things. I would need a fire, and I would need to take care of the wound.

I had no gun, but I did have a knife, and I had matches. What else? Very little. A bit of tobacco, but no food. No matter, if I could find Apache I'd have both a gun and food.

Water. I needed water to replace the blood I'd lost, and to bathe my wound. With water and a fire I stood a chance. It took an effort, but after a couple of tries I was able to stand. A wave of dizziness swept over me, but eased after a few minutes.

I found a small stream less than a hundred yards away, and dropped gratefully to my belly, sucking in the water until I could drink no more. Sitting up, I wiped water from my mouth with the sleeve of my jacket.

It was then I saw the wolves. Just one at first, standing in the brush thirty yards away, curious eyes locked on mine. Then a second wolf appeared. Soon more than a dozen wolves milled about in the brush, and they were moving closer.

Standing up, I walked along the stream until I found a spot where a large tree overhung the cold water. Quickly gathering all the wood nearby, I built a fire. The wolves didn't leave, but they did retreat a little farther into the darkness.

Bathing my wound and washing blood from my hair in cold water, I removed my jacket, ripped the sleeve from my shirt, and used that as a bandage for my head. The image reflecting back at me from the water was far from pretty, but it was the reflection of a living man, and that was the important thing.

Hunger bit at my belly, but there was nothing to be done for it. Rolling a cigarette, I lit it, inhaled deeply, thought of Charlie and the others. Paul was dead. The arrows in his back were centered and buried deep.

But what of the others? Had Charlie and Billy been killed as well?

I didn't know, and that bothered me far more than my own trouble.

Who attacked us, and why? Paul was killed by arrows,

and that meant Indians. Or did it? It was a white man who shot me. I saw him clearly. A white man, and no doubt about it. That didn't mean they were all white men, of course. Indians might have been working with them, or one of the white men might have been handy with a bow and used it to kill Paul quietly.

There were too many question without answers. Come morning, I would go looking for the truth, but right then I needed rest. Gathering enough wood to last the night, I built up the fire, curled up into as comfortable a position as was possible under the circumstances, and went to sleep.

It was deep into the night when something woke me up. As I sat up, the sound of a savage battle came to my ears. It was a battle of fang and claw, of wolf against something else equally savage, equally brutal.

For half an hour the battle raged, fierce growls and snarls mixed with sudden, horrible cries of pain. Then the battle ended and silence filled the night. Who had won? Were the wolves victors or vanquished? And what in God's name had they been fighting? What, outside of a bear, could put up a fight like that?

Something moved in the darkness. Only a whisper of sound, but when I heard it again it was much closer. Then a pair of red eyes appeared. They were wide apart, well up from the ground, and belonged to something big.

My knife was in my hand, but it seemed woefully inadequate against whatever that thing was. Picking up a long, heavy stick intended for the fire, I watched the pair of glowing red eyes and waited. The eyes moved closer and a shape formed around them. For just a moment I thought it was a wolf, then realized it couldn't be. The head was shaped wrong, the body too large and powerful.

A dog. It had to be a dog. The biggest, meanest-looking dog on the face of the earth, maybe, but still a dog.

It moved a half dozen steps closer in the space of a few seconds, then froze in the firelight. For a moment we stared into each other's eyes. It was a mastiff, like the dog I'd petted in the cage back on the dock at Skagway.

"It's all right, boy," I said soothingly. "It's all right."

At the sound of my voice the dog lowered its head a little and whined. It was not a whine of fear, but of hope. Putting the knife back in the scabbard, I held out my hand. The dog approached slowly and extended its nose, sniffing at my hand. After I gained his confidence he was all over me, rubbing against me, whining and barking.

The dog weighed considerably more than I did, and for a minute I was an unwilling captive beneath it. But there was no harm intended, and when I pushed, the dog moved off me. Stroking it behind the ear, I noticed the wounds for the first time.

A pair of gashes lined the dog's right shoulder, and a half dozen more marked the face. There was a deep nick in the left rear leg, and one ear was torn.

None of the wounds were serious, but each had bled and was certainly painful. "Those wolves must have given you a pretty hard time," I said. "Guess you gave more than you got, though, or you wouldn't be here."

I cleaned the dog's wounds as best I could. "Guess it's just you and me, boy," I said. "Come morning we'll go out and tackle the world."

I laid back down and the dog curled up tight against me. The warmth of its body felt good in the cold of the night. With that warmth soaking into me, and with the knowledge that the dog would warn me if we had unexpected visitors, I slept better than I had any right to.

When morning came, I built the fire higher and sat there, trying to think. I had the worst headache of my life, but the dizziness was gone, and it seemed I would live. Or at least I wouldn't die from the bullet wound. But without a gun and a horse, I might well die from something else.

The dog was still with me and showed no inclination to leave. That was something. Probably the only thing he couldn't handle would be a full-grown grizzly, and he might even frighten one of those away.

He needed a name. I couldn't keep calling him "dog." He deserved better. But what to call him? He was sitting up and staring at me as I thought, and now and again he would kind of cock his head to the left, an inquisitive look on his face. When he did that it reminded me of an uncle I had back in Kentucky.

Jack Hiram was his name, but we just called him Uncle Jack, and so did most of the folks who knew him. Anyway, Uncle Jack had that same habit of cocking his head to one side whenever you were talking to him. "How does the name Jack suit you?" I asked. "On formal occasions we can call you Uncle Jack."

Jack didn't answer, exactly, but he did cock his head to one side and bark. "Good," I said. "It's settled. From now on your name is Jack."

Having a name for him was all well and good, but taking time to think of one was just a way of avoiding more serious problems, and I knew it. Jack could kill his own food and protect himself against almost anything. But that probably wasn't going to help me much. I needed food and I needed a gun, or I was going to be easy pickings for anything bigger and stronger that came along.

And yet, as much as I wanted and needed those things, there was one thing I needed more. I needed to know if Charlie and Billy were dead or alive. That was my first priority.

But I wasn't at all certain of where I was, or where the camp was in relation to me. It seemed unlikely that Apache could have carried me far before I fell from the saddle. A mile perhaps? Two miles? I remembered crawling, but surely that wouldn't have added much to the distance.

All I could do was make a circle and try to pick up the tracks Apache must have left. They would lead me back to camp, and I might find Apache in the process.

Standing up, I reached down and patted Jack on the head. "Come on, Jack. Let's go find my friends."

It proved not to be that easy. Finding a spot of high ground, I looked at the surrounding country, but recognized nothing. With Jack by my side, and a long stick in my right hand, I started walking a long, wide, circle.

A quarter mile farther on, we found hoofprints, and it wasn't hard to see they belonged to Apache. Hoping to find him, I started along in the direction they were going. Another half mile down the trail I saw Apache standing in the open, head down, one hoof held off the ground.

Speaking in a soft, comforting voice, I worked my way closer. His breathing was raspy, coarse, and he didn't move when I took the reins. Patting him gently on the neck, I moved around to the off side. Blood. He was covered with blood seeping from a bullet hole behind his shoulder. That's why his breathing was so raspy, and why he didn't have the strength to raise his head.

I felt tears coming to my eyes. "Damn it, Apache," I said. "Why couldn't you have moved just a little faster? Another inch and that bullet would've hit the saddle and probably stopped before it hurt you.

"I'll get the man who did this, Apache. I swear to God, I'll put a bullet in him and watch him die."

Crying like a baby, I stripped saddle and gear from Apache. Only a minute later he dropped to his knees, then onto his side. My rifle was in the scabbard on the saddle and I pulled it free, levered a round into the chamber.

"I'm sorry, Apache," I said. "You were the best horse a man ever rode."

I shot Apache through the head, and he never twitched. For a minute I stood there, looking at Apache and listening to the echo of the shot reverberate across the wide country. Then I hid the saddle and covered it as best I could in case there was a chance to return for it later.

Taking only my saddlebags, blanket roll, and rifle, I started backtracking Apache.

Jack came along, sometimes following at my heels, sometimes ranging a hundred yards ahead, but never out of sight. We covered a mile, then most of another one. My head hurt from the bullet wound, and my stomach ached from hunger.

And I was seven kinds of a fool! I had some two-day-old biscuits and a hunk of moose meat in one of my saddlebags. Dropping onto the first large rock I saw, I jerked open the saddlebags and pulled out the food.

Three of the biscuits went down my throat in less than a minute, and I followed that with a big piece of meat.

The truth is, that meat smelled a bit iffy, but I ate half of it anyway, then tossed the rest to Jack. He swallowed it almost without chewing, and I tossed him a biscuit. That, too, disappeared down his throat.

Washing everything down with cold water from a nearby stream, I felt like a new man.

Then I heard three quick rifle shots from somewhere up ahead. I froze in my tracks. The shots were too far away to pose any threat to me, but judging just how far was difficult. Under the right conditions you can hear the sound of a rifle shot from a mile away, sometimes even a bit farther. Other times, when the wind is wrong and the air is hot and light, you can't hear a shot fired from three hundred yards.

These shots came from at least half a mile up the trail. Firing three quick shots is the traditional way to let anyone within hearing range know you need help.

Then shots rang out again. Two quick shots, four unpaced shots, then a flurry of gunfire.

This wasn't a hunter. A poor shot might take three or four rounds to either kill something or scare it away, but no more than that. It wasn't someone signaling for help, either.

It sounded like a gun battle. And that might mean Billy or Charlie was involved in whatever was happening. Our camp was somewhere up ahead, and this part of the Yukon was long on wild and short on people.

"Stay close, Jack," I said. "We need to work our way into this carefully."

Jack seemed to understand and stayed right at my heels as I moved slowly ahead, keeping to the thickest cover I could find. It took us an hour and a half of careful travel before we reached a spot where I could overlook the source of the shots.

What I saw was an empty meadow where our cattle had been, and beyond that I saw our camp. Three horses were ground-reined near the camp, and three men were behind the rocks to the north of our fire. Each man held a rifle, and they were all looking up the slope.

Two of the men fired several rapid shots up the slope. I was sitting a hundred yards from the nearest man, and a bit higher up, but I heard him when he cupped his hands around his mouth and yelled.

"Why don't you boys give it up?" he yelled. "You can't stay up there forever. We got food, water, and time. All you got is mosquitoes."

"Go to hell," a voice I recognized as Billy's answered.

So Billy, at least, was still alive. "All right, Jack," I said softly, "let's go down there and see if I can handle two-legged wolves as well as you handle four-legged ones."

CHAPTER 16

A JUTTING POINT of thick trees came to within thirty yards of our camp, and with luck I might be able to get that close without being seen. My hope was to come up behind the men and get the drop on them. That was my best, and maybe my only, chance of taking on all three men.

But the men were several yards apart, and there were large rocks and even boulders all around the area where they stood watching the slope. If I was careless, or if one or two of them made it to the other side of the rocks, I'd have a fight on my hands.

At first I hoped that Billy might give me help. If the men moved around the rocks to escape me, they would have to expose themselves to Billy's field of fire. That hope was dashed when Billy fired a shot down the slope. It came from a pistol, and the bullet bounced off a rock thirty yards short of the men.

If Billy had a rifle he wouldn't be taking potshots with a short gun. He wasn't going to be much help.

And Jack worried me as well. I wanted to leave him behind, but there was no way he would obey an order like that. He simply wouldn't understand it. I was afraid he would give my position away as I stalked to get behind the men. I was also afraid he would get himself shot if a gunfight broke out.

But there was nothing for it. I had to get down there, and Jack was obviously going with me.

I'll say this for him, Jack seemed to know something serious was about to happen. He stayed close by my side as

I stalked through the woods, he didn't bark, and he made less noise moving through the thick trees than I did.

You move slow making a stalk like that, the slower the better. One false move, one step on a dry stick, and you've given yourself away. And the faster you move, the easier you are to see. Peripheral vision picks up movement even better than straight-ahead vision does.

It took us better than an hour to cover the hundred yards between where we started and where the jut of trees ended thirty yards behind the men. Jack had been right at my side for the whole hour, but when I stopped at the end of the jut and looked down, he was gone.

I scanned the woods, the clearing, the rocks, without seeing him. I couldn't worry about it.

The men were there, thirty yards away, their backs exposed to me. When I thought of Paul lying dead in the trees, and when I thought of Apache, it was tempting to just start shooting. Instead, I stepped into the open, rifle ready, and walked closer to the men.

I made ten yards before one of them turned and saw me. His eyes went wide and he yelled. All three men started to turn. "Don't try it," I said. "Drop the rifles. Now!"

I thought they were going to do it. All three rifles started to lower, and I thought they were going to give it up. Then one of the men suddenly spun the rest of the way around, bringing his rifle to his shoulder. Swinging the front sight his way, I fired the moment it centered on his chest. The bullet caught him, spun him around.

Levering another round into the chamber, I swung back to the first man. Our shots crossed each other. Something hot snapped past my face without doing harm. My bullet took the man's leg out from under him, and he went down, dropping the rifle.

The third man was gone. When I swung the rifle his way, he simply wasn't there. Where was he? Behind the rocks? Almost certainly. Was he moving? To the left or the right? Where was he?

I wanted to dart for cover, but any way I ran might be the wrong way and I had a wounded man in front of me who still had a Colt in his holster.

The trees ten yards behind me offered the quickest route to cover, but if I moved back in there we could have a standoff that might last for days. The line of boulders along the far side of the camp, where the man was hidden, was the place I wanted to be. It was dangerous, yes, but it was my best chance to force him into the open.

Keeping my rifle in the ready position, I walked toward the boulders, well to the right of where the third man disappeared. As I walked, I yelled to the wounded man.

"Throw your Colt away, then the rifle. Do it now."

Clutching his wounded leg, he glared at me, but didn't move. I pulled the trigger and the rifle roared. The bullet struck within inches of his body, kicking dirt and grass high in the air. "Do it now," I said.

He pulled the pistol free of the holster and tossed it well away. The rifle had fallen just beyond his reach, but he scooted to it, grabbed it by the barrel and slung it ten yards. "Good," I said. "Now sit still and you might live through this."

Reluctantly taking my eyes off the man, I started the last ten yards toward the boulders. Too late. As I turned, the third man was already standing there, rifle leveled.

He was thirty yards away, a good bit to my left, and my rifle was out of line. I swung the barrel his way, knowing I was going to be too late.

A tenth of a second before he fired, Jack leaped through the air at him and he went down. The rifle exploded in the air, the bullet sailing harmlessly away. In falling, the man had dropped behind a boulder, but he was screaming. His screams were mixed with Jack's savage growling.

Running to the boulder, I stepped behind it just in time

to see Jack lock his huge jaws down on the man's throat. The man's scream turned into a horrible gurgling sound; his eyes were wide, filled with terror and pleading. His hands beat at Jack, but there was no strength left in them.

Grabbing Jack, I pulled at his huge body. "That's enough, Jack. Let go. That's enough."

The dog reluctantly eased his grip on the man's throat and backed away, his fangs still snapping together and a steady snarling growl coming from his chest.

It was too late to save the man. His throat was ripped wide open and blood gushed everywhere. He clawed at his neck as if trying to stop the flow of blood. In less than a minute his eyes fluttered, and the bleeding stopped.

Few men die a more horrible death, and I wanted to feel sorry for him, but it wasn't in me. He had brought this on himself.

I yelled up the slope, and after a moment Billy yelled back, "Kerrigan, is that you?"

"It's me. Are you all right?"

Billy stood up before yelling. "I'm all right, but Charlie's hurt pretty bad. You better get up here."

I walked over to the wounded bushwhacker. He'd taken his belt off and was using it for a tourniquet, pulling it tight around his bad leg to stop the flow of blood. "You got to get me help," he said, "or I'm gonna bleed to death."

"I have to go up there and see how a friend of mine is doing, and I'm not about to leave you down here with the horses and the guns. So get up and start hobbling up the slope."

"What? Mister, you're crazy. I can't walk. I got a bullet in my leg."

"You walk, or hop, or crawl," I said, "but get moving or you'll have a bullet somewhere else."

I punctuated my order by thumbing back the hammer of my Winchester. He cursed loud enough to wake the dead, but he stood up and started hopping. Halfway up the slope he fell. Thinking we were far enough from the horses and guns, I let him stay where he was.

"If you move one inch back down the slope," I said, "I'll put a bullet in you and leave you for the wolves."

Jack was following us, staying twenty yards or so behind, but when the man fell he moved up close to us. The hair around his mouth and most of his chest was still covered with blood from the man he'd killed. Between that and the scabbed-over gashes he had from the fight with the wolves, he was a fearsome-looking beast.

"Or better yet," I said to the man, "I'll just let Jack have you."

The man looked at Jack. Jack growled intuitively. The man turned two shades whiter.

Going on up the slope to where Billy waited, I saw Charlie lying behind a boulder. His back was against the rock and his eyes were closed. His side was stained with blood. His eyes opened as I knelt down beside him.

"Don't let Billy worry you none," he said. "I'm fine. Or I will be after I drink about a gallon of water."

Billy's sleeve was bloody, but he said it was only a scratch, so I let him go back down the slope for a canteen of water. "You sure that bear of yours won't take my leg off?" he asked.

"Jack? He won't bother you if you don't bother him."

Billy shook his head and walked down the slope, giving Jack wide berth. Jack watched him all the way down and back, but never left the wounded man.

Billy returned with the canteen and handed it to me. Tilting it up for Charlie, I let him drink a bit. "Take it slow," I said. "You can drink all you want, but a little at a time."

Opening Charlie's shirt, I saw the wound. The bullet had gone in just above the belt, bored through a few inches of skin and muscle, and exited. "You're a lucky old coot," I said. "I've cut myself worse than that shaving."

"That's what I been tryin' to tell Billy," Charlie said. "But he's been ready to read me the last rites ever since it happened."

"I am going to have to clean it out. If it gets infected it still could kill you."

We got Charlie to his feet, and with one of his arms around my shoulder and the other around Billy, we got him down to the camp. As we passed the wounded man he yelled at me. "What about me?" he said. "You just gonna let me sit here and bleed to death?"

"Mister," I said, "when I get everything else taken care of, I'll have a look at your leg . . . if you're still alive. In the meantime, sit still and shut up."

Rummaging through the saddlebags on the three horses, I found a bottle of whiskey, about a pound of jerky, and assorted odds and ends of food. Whoever drove the cattle off had taken our pack mules and supplies along with them, leaving just enough to last their three buddies a few days at most.

In the saddlebags of the last horse I found my Colt and slipped it into the holster. I took the blanket rolls from the horses and walked over to the fire. "Got to give those three one thing," Billy said. "They gathered enough wood to keep this fire going for a month."

"Put on a pot of water and let it boil," I said. "While we're waiting I'll take inventory of the supplies."

About all that remained of the men's supplies were three pounds of dried beans, some flour, and a five-pound slab of salt pork. We were all hungry, so I cut the salt pork into thick slices and filled two skillets. While the food was cooking, the water started to boil.

One of the men had a clean white shirt in his blanket roll, and I tore it into strips. Most of the strips I laid aside for bandages, but I dropped several into the boiling water for a minute, then hooked one of the wet, hot strips onto the end of a thin, freshly peeled stick.

I went over to Charlie and helped him take off his shirt. "This is going to hurt," I said. "You want some whiskey before I do it?"

Charlie took the bottle and swallowed three long drinks. "That's enough," he said. "Go ahead and get 'er done."

Pouring whiskey into the wound first, I worked the stick into the hole, letting it pull the strip of wet cloth along with it. Charlie gritted his teeth and his body stiffened. I worked the stick through to the exit hole and pulled the cloth through the wound, pouring whiskey on it all the while. Charlie was sweating like he'd been shoveling coal in the hot sun by the time I finished.

"If I ever get shot again," he said, "just go ahead and finish me off. I don't believe I want to go through that twice."

"It's your own fault for getting yourself shot," I said. "Duck next time."

"Duck, hell," Charlie said. "It happened too quick."

"It was you riding down to check on Paul that saved our lives," Billy said. "Whoever shot at you gave us about three seconds to dive for cover. We almost made it."

"We'd have been fine," Charlie said, "if we could have reached cover with our rifles, but mine was too far away, and Billy dropped his when that bullet nicked his arm.

"There were seven men in the bunch that hit us, and they sure tore things up trying to nail us before we could reach cover. We worked our way up the slope to where you found us, but that was it. Couldn't get no farther without coming into the open."

"Paul was killed by arrows," I said. "Did they have an Indian along?"

"One of them waved a bow around a good bit," Billy said. "He was dressed like a white man, but he wore an odd hat. It was black and had a flat brim. He could've been an Indian, I reckon."

"We thought they'd killed you, too," Charlie said.

"It was close," I said. "Too close."

"You left here with a horse and came back with a dog," Billy said. "How'd that come about?"

Taking a deep breath, I told them the story. When I finished there was silence for a time, then Billy spoke. "I'm sure sorry about your horse," he said. "A man don't find a good horse very often."

"No, sir," I said. "Not often."

The wounded fellow was still sitting up on the slope, and I hauled him down to camp. As I cut away his pant leg he fussed and cursed. "Mister," I said, "you want this hole plugged, shut up. You say one more thing I don't like and you can fix your own leg."

He shut up until I had his leg cleaned and bandaged, then started swearing again. I backhanded him just hard enough to rattle his teeth. "You're pressing it, mister. Keep a civil tongue in your head. While we're at it, I'm going to ask you a few questions, and if I even think you're lying to me, I'll make you regret it. Understand?"

He looked into my eyes. Whatever he saw there wasn't to his liking. "What do you want to know?"

"How many men in your bunch?"

He wet his lips. "Thirteen."

"So that leaves ten—where are they taking the cattle?"

"I don't know for sure . . . honest. The boss was going to drive them somewhere and keep them for a couple of weeks, then bring them out and sell 'em to one of the mining camps."

"Who's your boss?"

He didn't answer.

"Jack," I said, "come here, boy."

Jack trotted over beside me. "They say a dog bite hurts worse than almost anything," I said. "Worse than a burn, some say. Of course, not many live to talk about it."

The truth is, I had no idea how well Jack had been trained, whether he even would attack on command without sensing some threat to his safety or mine. But the wounded man did not call my bluff.

"Cu—Curly Joe Blake is boss out here. He answers to Soapy Smith."

"Where were you supposed to meet them?"

"We weren't. We were to follow along and catch up when we were done here. Curly said he'd send some boys back to help out if we took too long."

"One last question," I said. I pointed to the horse where I found my Colt. "Which one of you owns that horse?"

"Huh? Tabby over there owned it, the one you shot."

Apache was paid for, then, but it didn't satisfy me. The man died too fast and too easy.

"You got a name?" I asked.

"Sure. It's Selby. Dick Selby. Why?"

"Because if I find you've lied to me, even once, I need to know what name to carve on the headstone."

Tying the man's hands and feet, I scooted him far enough from the fire so we could talk without him hearing.

"Charlie," I asked, "how's your side?"

"It hurts, but I reckon I'll live."

"I mean, do we need to rush you to a doctor?"

Charlie spat. "Man runs to a doctor every time he gets a little hurt like this best move to a city and stay there.

"Sounds like you got something in mind. Want to let us in on it?"

"Ten at once is too many," I said. "If we wait here awhile we might be able to even the odds a little more."

"You mean when ol' Curly sends some boys back to check on these fellows? Now that's an idea. We do it right and they won't know what hit them."

"That's how I see it. Most of them should stay with the cattle, so we won't be up against more than three or four, likely. If we catch them by surprise, it should be easy."

"Let's do it," Billy said. "Paul was a good friend of mine, and I want a chance to even the score."

CHAPTER 17

SELBY CLAIMED NOT to know how long it would be until some of his friends came to see what was taking them so long. "Curly just said he'd send 'em after a time. Didn't say how long. We figured two or three days."

It was already near the end of the second day since the attack. Selby's friends might come along at any minute . . . or they might not come for days. Either way, we had to be ready.

Selby was close to my size, so I took his jacket and hat, hoping that when seen from a distance I would be mistaken for him. Charlie and Billy took jackets and hats from the two dead men, but the jackets were bloodstained and had to be washed out in the stream.

We hid the bodies of the dead men, and after tying and gagging Selby, stashed him in the rocks where he couldn't be seen by his friends.

"What about the fire?" Billy asked. "Do we put it out?"

"No, keep it going," I said. "Big and bright. When those boys come along we want them to think everything is fine. In fact, we should fire a few shots up toward that slope every now and then."

"Good idea," Charlie said. "They'll hear the shots from half a mile away an' think we're still pinned down up there."

"That's my hope."

"How long you plannin' on waitin' here?" Billy asked. "No telling when they'll have a chance to sell the cattle."

"They're weeks from any real market," I said. "But you're right, I don't want to stay here forever. We'll give them two days, maybe three. If no one shows by then, we'll have to go looking for them."

We settled down to wait. Nothing happened that evening, or all of the next day. Twice an hour we would fire a few shots up the slope, using the rifles belonging to the dead men.

Food became a problem. We were nearly out, in fact, so at dawn the next morning Billy slipped out through the woods in search of something to shoot. He killed a caribou, skinned it, and was carrying back a haunch when the riders showed up.

Billy was in that same jut of trees I'd used to get close to the camp, and when he saw the riders he dropped the meat, hunkered down next to a tree, and lined his rifle sights on the closest man.

Charlie saw them coming before I did, and as planned, he slipped over into the rocks where they couldn't see him. Pulling the jacket up around my neck, and the hat down against it, I turned my back on the coming riders, leaned against a boulder, and fired four shots up the slope at the spot where Charlie and Billy had been.

The bullets kicked up rock dust and ricocheted away with an ugly whining sound. I slipped four fresh cartridges into the rifle. The sound of horses grew nearer, then a man spoke up, seeming only yards away.

"Damn it, Selby," the voice said, "ain't you got them bastards out of the rocks yet? Where the hell are Bob and Tabby, anyway?"

I turned around, levering a cartridge into the chamber and stopping the muzzle swing on the first man I saw.

"Bob and Tabby are both in hell," I said. "You can join them, if you like."

You never saw a more surprised bunch of men. There were four of them, and all four dropped their jaws wide when they realized I wasn't Selby.

"What's going on here?" one of them asked. "Where's our friends?"

"I already told you, they're in hell playing cards with the devil. You want in on the game, just make a move I don't like."

One of them tried. He grabbed for his Colt, and I squeezed the trigger. Billy fired from the woods and Charlie put in his two cents' worth from the rocks. All of our shots came within half a second of each other, and the man who tried to grab his Colt was simply thrown from the saddle, dead before he hit the ground.

Those other three turned meek. They dropped their guns and we made quick work of tying them up.

"That lowers the odds a good bit," Charlie said. "If Selby was tellin' the truth, that leaves just six men with the cattle."

"Uh-huh," Billy said, "but what are we gonna do with these fellows? We can't leave 'em here, and we sure can't take 'em with us to chase the herd."

It was a point we hadn't considered. All we had been concerned about was cutting the odds. What came after never entered our minds.

"I don't know what to do with them," I said. "Any ideas, Charlie?"

"I got an idea, all right," he said. "Let's shoot 'em and go after the cattle."

Charlie's shirt still bore the bloodstain from his wound, his beard was scraggly, and his eyes were cold. Those men looked at him, and there wasn't a doubt in their minds that he would shoot them and not lose a minute's sleep over it.

"That's what I'd like to do," Charlie said, "but I guess we can't. There's a mounted police checkpoint over on the Yukon River. That's maybe three days' travel from here."

It was all we could think of to do with them. "I guess

that's it," I said. "Though shooting them is sounding better all the time."

"It does at that," Charlie said. "It's at least three days to that checkpoint, and three days back. Throw in a few more days to find the cattle, and we might be out of luck.

"When these boys don't get back, ol' Curly might get to wonderin' what happened to them. If he wonders too hard, he might just sell the cattle at the first place he finds . . . or scatter them and take off for Skagway. If he does that, we'll be up the creek without a paddle."

With tobacco taken from the men, I rolled a cigarette, struck a match to the end, and tried to think of a way out. Only one came to mind.

"Charlie, can you and Billy get these fellows to the Mounties without me?"

"Sure. But what're you planning to do while we're gone?"

"There isn't a way in the world they can hide the tracks all those cattle make," I said, "and they can't push them more than fifteen miles a day. Probably less. I think I'll ride along and catch up with the herd. Maybe I can keep Curly and his boys busy until you bring in some help."

"There's still six of them," Billy said, "and one of you. That's long odds."

"I'm not about to fight them," I said. "But I might take a potshot or two, if the chance comes. The shoe is on the other foot now. They have to watch the cattle, and I'll be free to run the woods. At best they won't be able to send more than three or four men after me, and I won't wait. I'll take a shot or two, then run. Might be I can keep them from doing anything with the herd that way."

"You might," Charlie said, "but you're takin' a big risk. I'd hate to lose those cattle, but I don't want you killed over 'em."

"I'll be fine. You just hustle these boys to the checkpoint

and get back as soon as possible. I won't take any chances while you're gone."

"You'll pardon me if I don't believe that," Charlie said. "But it's not a bad idea, at that."

With everything decided, we packed up the camp and made ready to move. Stripping their horses of everything useful, we tied the prisoners tightly and put them in the saddle. Selby cursed a blue streak at having to ride with a wounded leg. I just smiled at him.

The horse I picked for myself was a big buckskin that looked to have speed and staying power. He wasn't Apache, but he was a fine horse. Too good for the man who'd owned him.

Charlie and Billy rode off with the prisoners toward the Yukon River, and with Jack tagging along for company, I started back along the trail of the men we'd captured. They paralleled the trail left by the herd, and after studying that for a time, I knew the men who rustled them weren't cowboys.

They were pushing the herd too hard, and they weren't taking time to scout ahead and find the easiest trail. If they didn't slow down they were going to run a lot of weight off the cattle, and if they didn't pick better routes, they were going to lose a few head.

They didn't do either. I found the first dead steer after five miles on the trail. It had wandered into a bog and they'd let it stay there to die.

The cattle had been stolen almost four days earlier, and if the thieves pushed them all the way at the same pace, it meant I might be as much as fifty miles from the herd. But I doubted that was the case. It was more likely they would only push the cattle until they found a good place to hold them for a while. How far along the trail that would be remained to be seen.

I rode slow, not wanting to blunder into anything. That evening I made camp well before dark, and put a chunk of caribou meat over the fire to roast. I had coffee taken from the prisoners, and a pot of that went over the fire as well.

The mosquitoes were still thick, but somehow we'd adjusted to them after a time. Sitting there around the fire, drinking coffee and eating caribou meat, I listened to them humming around my ears. Now and then I'd have to swat one, but for the most part the smoke from the fire kept them at bay.

As darkness fell there was a chill in the air that bothered me. Charlie was the expert on this far north country, and I had no idea how early winter came on, but the air felt like summer was on the way out.

Even if we got the cattle back, we were going to be another couple of weeks behind schedule, and the likelihood of having to spend a winter in Alaska was getting more and more likely.

White Pass was low and rough. It wouldn't take much snow to make it impassable. The Chilkoot, however, could be crossed in almost any weather, but it had to be done on foot. Still, winters on the coast were supposed to be quite a bit milder than winters in the interior, so if we did have to spend the winter, then Skagway was the place to do it.

Crawling under my blankets not long after dark, I went to sleep without any effort at all. Jack was snuggled in close by my side, and he was better than a fire for keeping a man warm.

But right in the middle of the night he woke me up by suddenly barking right in my ear, and if you think a dog that big doesn't bark loud, you're wrong. Still groggy with sleep, I sat up and grabbed my rifle. Jack was standing next to me, his legs stiff, his hair on end. He was barking and growling, looking into the darkness beyond the camp.

Looking that way, I dimly saw eyes glowing from the light of the dying campfire. I threw more wood onto the fire and it surged higher, the light it cast spreading deeper into the woods.

The eyes I'd been watching were three or four feet above the ground, but suddenly they rose straight up until they were ten feet in the air. A roar came from the direction of the eyes, and my stomach tightened into a knot. The eyes moved closer, came into the firelight, and I saw what I'd feared all along.

It was a bear. The biggest bear God ever made, by the look of it. The bear stood on its hind legs, and a scarier sight I've never seen.

Jack was going crazy, barking and growling in time with the even deeper growls coming from the bear. But Jack, big as he was, had more sense than to run in and tackle a grizzly. The rifle felt small and useless in my hands, but I slowly levered a round into the chamber and put the sights on the bear's head.

In the trees behind me I could hear my horse stomping the ground and whinnying, obviously frightened by the scent of the bear.

The last thing in the world I wanted to do was pull the trigger. If I missed, or if the shot didn't kill the bear, it would be all over us before I could fire again. But if it charged before I fired, hitting it would be that much harder. Reluctantly, I started taking up slack on the trigger.

At that moment the bear turned and dropped to all fours. It walked away from us, disappearing into the darkness within moments.

For better than an hour the bear moved around in the night, circling our camp and roaring. I moved my horse a bit closer and sat there next to Jack. The sounds of the bear eventually moved away, but it was at least a couple of hours after that before I felt safe enough to sleep.

Because of the excitement with the bear, I slept a little later than normal, and when I awoke it was full light. Jack was sitting not far away, chewing on the remains of a rabbit.

"Looks like you couldn't wait for breakfast," I said. "Or maybe you just don't like my cooking?"

Jack woofed out an answer. "Well," I said, "the truth is I don't much care for it myself. Guess I can't blame you for wanting fresh rabbit over old caribou."

After breakfast we started along the trail again, but it was starting to look like another day would pass without catching the herd. Then, as darkness approached and I was looking for a place to camp, a steer walked to the top of a small hill about six hundred yards away.

Cutting my horse into cover, I stopped and watched the steer. It was a long ways off, but silhouetted against the evening sky and easy to see. Was it a stray, or part of the herd? I didn't know.

Then a rider appeared near the steer and drove it back down the other side of the hill.

"Looks like we found what we're looking for," I said to Jack. "Now all we have to do is figure out what to do about it."

CHAPTER 18

IT WAS LATE, and I wanted a chance to eat and plan before moving closer to the herd, so the first thing I did was turn away and ride almost a mile to the east. Only when I found a place far enough away from the men to build a fire without worry did I stop.

The site had trees, boulders, and rolling ground to block the light of the fire, and it had thick foliage above to break up the smoke. But I built the fire small and kept it that way, not wanting to take any chances.

I drank coffee, ate, and thought. My plan was to harass the men holding the herd, force them to worry about me rather than the cattle. If they could be stopped from making a quick sale somewhere, and stopped from scattering the herd to hell and gone, we had them.

Charlie and Billy would get the men to the mounted police and return as soon as possible, but how soon would that be? Charlie said three days each way, plus at least two more days to follow me to the herd. So it would be a minimum of eight days before help would come. It might take longer.

That was a long, long time to keep the men around the herd busy. I would have to hit and run, and run was the key word.

Jack was a problem. He might come in handy if trouble came, but he might also give me away at a bad time. So far, he'd shown signs of intelligence, and of training. Someone at some point had taken pains to train Jack well. Of that I was certain.

But I still didn't know him well enough to judge how he would react in some situations.

The thought came to me that tying him to a tree two or three miles from the herd might be the wisest choice. I could give him plenty of rope to run on so he could defend himself if attacked, and I could check on him every now and then to make sure he was all right.

After several cups of coffee, I decided it was time to go look in on the herd. Taking the rope from my saddle, I walked over to Jack. "I sure hope you like this idea," I said, "because you're too big to fight."

Jack cocked his head to one side and barked twice. He never flinched when I slipped the rope over his neck. The rope was an inch or more thick and fifty feet long. With one end around Jack's neck, and the other end tied to a tree, he shouldn't have a problem taking care of himself if trouble came.

He pulled at the rope a couple of times, testing its length and strength, then lay down, calm as you please. Crossing his front feet, he rested his chin on them and watched me with sad eyes as I rode off into the night.

I rode away from Jack at a walk, and I hoped that was as fast as we had to go the rest of the night. All I wanted to do was get a look at the thieves' camp and map it out in my mind. If an opportunity came along to give them some grief, I'd take it, but that wasn't the main objective.

Roughly speaking, I knew the location of the camp, so I circled to the west, aiming for a hill overlooking it from two hundred yards away. There was a full moon, but in the trees the shadows were deep and dark. We went along a step at a time, not caring how long it took to get there.

When we reached the back side of the hill I reined to a stop and slid from the saddle. Looping the reins around a low tree limb, I patted the horse on the neck. "All right, Buck," I said. "You keep out of trouble. I won't be gone long."

Rifle in hand, I went up the hill and flattened out at the top, moving on my belly to a spot that overlooked the camp. It was seventy-five yards farther west, and a good bit closer to the hill than I'd anticipated. My location put me almost directly above the fire, and maybe sixty yards away.

Those boys had a good-sized fire going, and their blankets nearly surrounded it. I counted only four horses picketed at the far side of the camp. Only three men sat around the fire.

The cattle were in a clearing east and north of the fire, and I watched them for several minutes. At last I saw a rider, little more than a shape in the night, circling the herd in a clockwise motion. A few minutes later I saw a second rider circling the herd in the opposite direction.

All right, two men on guard around the cattle, three around the fire. One man was missing. All six horses were accounted for, so the man was on foot. But where?

Moonlight glinted off something in the brush not far from the camp, and I locked my eyes on the spot. At first I saw nothing. Then a man stepped from the shadow and into the light. He was wearing a grayish coat that seemed a part of the darkness, and there was something odd about the shape of his hat, but just what eluded me.

The man walked to the fire and sat down, giving me a better look at him. His hat was black and had a flat brim. That's what threw me about its shape. If a man doesn't curl the brim of his hat upward, rain will soon bend it down. But the brim on this man's hat was flat and stiff as a board. Charlie said the man who'd waved the bow and bragged about killing Paul wore a hat like this one.

The firelight glinted off something hanging about the man's neck, but from the distance there was no telling what the object was. The man had been holding a cup of coffee, and he was looking down at it, as a man will when thinking about one thing or another.

Without warning he lifted his head and looked right at

me. I was better than sixty yards away, lying in the deep shadow and well above the fire. There was no possible way he could see me. Yet his eyes locked on me and stayed there. I was afraid to move.

The man's face was dark in the firelight, and his cheekbones stood out plain. He never moved at all except to raise his cup for a sip once, and all the while his eyes stayed locked on my position.

Had he seen me? It shouldn't have been possible, but if he couldn't see me, why was he staring my way so intently? Had something given me away as it had him? Could the moonlight have glinted off something of mine as it had that object around his neck?

I slowly looked down at myself to see if there was something on or around me that might show up in the dark. The check was a quick one, taking no more than two or three seconds, but when I looked back down the hill toward the fire, the man was gone.

I went down the back side of the hill at a dead run, jerked the reins free, and hit the saddle all in one move. Buck knew what to do, and lit out of there at a full gallop. But we hadn't made fifty yards when a rifle shot shattered the night. I heard the snap as the bullet cut the air near us.

Glancing back over my shoulder, I saw a man standing at the foot of the hill. Fire burst from his rifle, and another bullet came too close. Then we were into the trees and safe from the bullets.

When we came to the place I'd left Jack I didn't waste time. Whoever that man was, he was good. Too good. This camp was too close to theirs, and the trail we'd left would be too easy to follow. Making certain the fire was out, I cut Jack loose and rode away into the night.

Keeping to water or rock as much as possible to make my trail hard to follow, I also looped around twice, riding a wide figure eight.

The place where we finally stopped was three miles from the first camp, and high on the side of a ridge where I could see my backtrail, and a lot of other country besides.

Three hours' sleep was all I got, but it would have to be enough. Just before dawn I was in the saddle again, riding a wide circle to the northwest. Curly and his boys would know someone was watching them now, and there was no telling how they would react.

They might fort up and wait for me to make a move, they might try to get the cattle to a place where they could be quickly sold . . . or they might come looking for me. Whichever they did, I wanted to be ready, and to be ready, I had to know. If they moved the cattle, it would almost certainly be with the natural lay of the land, and probably toward the Stewart River.

They could sell a lot of cattle in a short time along that river. Not at Dawson prices, but still high enough to make more money than most of them would ever see otherwise.

I didn't know the country well enough. Not well enough at all. Every bit of knowledge I had came from talking to Charlie, plus a few men back in Skagway. But I did know cattle, and the kind of route they would need. That was all I had to work with, so I took a chance.

Riding to a spot of high ground about two miles northwest of the herd, I found a place where we couldn't easily be seen, and I waited. Jack took off during the ride, and when he returned an hour later there was blood around his mouth.

Sitting down under a tree, I petted Jack and looked out over the country. Just before noon a movement in the distance caught my eye. The movement grew, became walking cattle. They were pushing the herd toward the Stewart River, just as I feared.

Of the three things they might have done, that was probably the worst for me. Had they forted up, I could have simply waited for help to arrive. Had they come after me, I could have kept them chasing me for miles. Either way, the cattle would have been there waiting for the mounted police Charlie was hoping to bring.

But when they started pushing the cattle, it meant the next move was mine—I had to stop them, and that might not be easy.

Scratching Jack behind the ear, I stood up and walked to Buck. "Best thing you could do, Jack," I said, "would be to take off for Skagway and hop on the first ship out. Things may get rough from now on."

Riding to a site five hundred yards to the north, I found cover near a spot where the cattle would pass if those men down there knew their business. They didn't. Instead of running the cattle along a natural ridge, they pushed them up and over the top, saving some time, but causing two steers to fall on the rock.

It also took them three hundred yards farther away from me than I wanted. The shot I'd hoped for was something over two hundred yards, and at that distance I could hit anything I aimed at. The shot I was going to get was closer to six hundred yards, and that's well over a quarter of a mile.

It couldn't be helped. If I tried to move closer to get a better shot they might see me, and I'd be the target. So when the herd reached the point closest to my position, I thumbed back the hammer on my rifle, looked down the barrel, took a deep breath, let half of it out, then squeezed the trigger. The rifle barked, jumped in my hands.

A man grabbed his left arm and almost fell from the saddle. I emptied the rifle, picking out targets as quickly as possible. The second shot missed, the third knocked a horse down, and the last four did little damage, but made men hunt cover.

I took off, riding away from the herd as fast as Buck would take me. Fighting wasn't part of my plan. All I wanted to do was make them afraid to sit up in the saddle and drive cattle. Riding hard for a half hour, I came in on the herd from behind. They were driving the cattle again, so with a full rifle I tried to discourage them. I took out another horse, and its rider came close to getting trampled under a big bull when the horse somersaulted. He came to his feet and went up a tree like a squirrel, but it was safe to say he wasn't happy.

The second time worked. They wasted no time in finding a draw where the cattle couldn't roam far, and they made camp in the shelter of several large boulders. They were two horses short now, so a couple of men were going to have to walk wherever they went.

Not wanting to hang around and take a chance on any of them spotting me, I patted myself on the back and started to ride away. Right then two men left the camp, riding their horses hell-bent-for-leather due east. I watched for several minutes, thinking they might be planning to circle around and come in on my back.

But when they disappeared from sight they were still going due east and still riding at a gallup.

That bothered me, but there wasn't time to worry about it. I had to get out of there, cover my trail, and find a safe place to camp.

Three hours later I was building a small fire under the shelter of an overhanging rock. Trees grew to within twenty yards of the rock on three sides, and the last side was a steep, gravel-covered slope that a mouse couldn't cross without starting a small avalanche that would alert me.

I was getting low on food, so I worked a quick hunting trip into my plans. Half a mile to the southwest I killed a beaver who was chewing on a tree. Taking it back to camp, I skinned it out and roasted the meat over the fire.

I'd heard beaver tail was one of the finest tasting meats to be had, so I roasted that, too, and the stories were true. The meat was white, sweet, and almighty good.

With my belly full of food, coffee to settle it in place, and a cigarette to help me think, I leaned back and thought over the situation. There wasn't much about it that I liked. What bothered me most was wondering where those two yahoos were going when they rode off to the east.

Wherever it was, they were in a big hurry to get there. They must have been going to get help. Nothing else made sense. Somewhere to the east they had friends, and those two were going after them.

Keeping six men pinned down wasn't all that difficult, especially when they were two horses short and somebody had to keep the cattle from drifting, or from becoming a meal for wolves and bears. But if they brought back another six men, I was in trouble. Six more men could come hunting me, and if they knew the country and knew how to track, I'd play hob trying to stay away from them.

With this in mind, I crawled into my blankets, said goodnight to Jack, and went to sleep. Maybe my friends will get here first, I thought. Then I was dreaming of Angie.

CHAPTER 19

WITH THE HERD not moving and the cattle thieves seeming content to sit and wait, I did the same. Each day I would ride to the top of a high bluff a half mile from the herd. From there it was possible to see the cattle moving around, and that was all I wanted.

Five days passed in this way. I began watching the trail for Charlie and any help he might bring, but the trail remained empty. Then, on the sixth day, I rode up to the bluff and saw a dozen horses moving toward the camp.

Keeping to cover, I rode to a spot where I could see the camp itself. In doing so I more than cut the distance in half. Leaving Buck in a brushy draw, I slipped over to the edge of a slope where I could see the camp. It was crawling with men. Curly's friends had arrived before mine, and that was going to make things rough.

There looked to be an even dozen new men in the camp, plus two or three spare horses. That was too many. With that many men they could move the herd and still have plenty of guns to send after me.

"Charlie," I said aloud, "I don't know where you are, but this would be a good time for you to show up."

He didn't show up. Even as I watched, Curly and his men started breaking camp. Within twenty minutes everything was packed, and they were moving the cattle.

Stretched out on the grass, I tried to think things through. Curly knew someone was trying to keep him from moving the cattle, and he knew the men he'd left to kill Charlie and Billy hadn't returned; nor had the four men he sent to help them. He could only take that to mean they were dead or captive.

He had to be worried. If we had been killed, he could say he bought the cattle. But with any of us alive, especially Charlie, since the brand was registered to him, Curly had to unload the cattle fast. He had to take what he could get and run.

That meant he'd sell the cattle a few at a time along the Stewart River, or to any of the several dozen small mining camps in the Klondike. There was plenty of gold dust around, and plenty of hungry men. With luck he could sell every one of the cattle in a few days' time.

The question was, how could I stop him? I'd succeeded for six days, but there wasn't a thing I could do against eighteen men. Nothing except follow along at a safe distance and hope for something to happen that would give me an edge.

Easing back toward cover, I stood up. Before I could turn around a voice spoke right behind me. "Got you, by God," the voice said. "Lift your hands and turn around slow."

Raising my hands to shoulder height, I turned around, knowing who I was going to see. It was the man with the flat-brimmed hat. He was standing thirty feet away, a big Colt in his hand.

His face had seemed unusually dark in the firelight, and now I saw why. The man was an Indian, or a half-breed. Around his neck hung a silver and gold necklace, and the amulet on the end was in the shape of an odd-looking animal with horns. That was what I had seen the moonlight reflecting from.

Jack was tied up back at my camp, and I cursed myself for not bringing him along. No one could have moved up behind me if Jack had been there.

"Reach down with your left hand and unbuckle the gun belt," he said. "Give me any reason at all and I'll kill you."

I couldn't let him take me. I'd be a dead man anyway, the moment he got me back to Curly.

When a man is aiming a gun at you and his finger is on the trigger, it looks hopeless. But if he isn't going to shoot unless you give him reason, there's a chance. Not much of one, but a chance.

Moving my left hand very slowly downward, I took hold of the buckle on my gunbelt as if to unfasten it. At that instant I snapped my right hand down for my holstered Colt.

My thumb snapped off the leather thong holding the Colt in place, then cocked the hammer as my fingers curled around the butt. The heavy Colt was on the way up, the barrel almost clear of the holster, when his eyes widened slightly, and his finger pulled the trigger.

I saw the flame burst from his Colt, heard the roar, felt the slam of the bullet, all so close together it seemed instantaneous.

There was a roaring in my ears, but no pain. My own Colt leveled and jumped in my hand. A small bloodstain appeared on his chest, began to spread. Our second shots crossed, and again something jolted my body.

Through the roar in my ears, and through an odd haziness in front of my eyes, I saw the man stagger, drop to his knees. I fired twice more without conscious thought, and he fell forward, his face a mask of blood. For what seemed a long time I stood there, trying to think. Then I half-walked, half-staggered to my horse.

Getting in the saddle was a chore, but I made it on the third try. Leaning forward in the saddle, I rode away.

I was hurt, but I wasn't sure how bad. My mind told me that two bullets had struck me, but my whole body seemed numb.

Two thoughts came through the fog. They'll be coming after me now, and Jack is still tied up. Have to cut him loose.

The next thing I knew I was at my camp. Dropping from the saddle, I fell, stood up, found my knife, and cut the rope holding Jack to a tree. "You'd best go find somebody else to ride with," I said. "They're coming after me, and I'm not going to make it."

I stumbled to the ground and passed out.

Sometime later I opened my eyes. While I was unconscious, the shock of the wounds left me, and pain had set in. It hurt like hell to move, but it hurt almost as much to lie still, so I moved.

Staggering down to the stream, I stripped to the waist and examined myself. One bullet punched a hole through the muscle connecting the neck and shoulder, and the second bullet went in just below the collar bone on the same side. It was still in there, but I could move the arm and rotate the shoulder. A wave of agony went through me when I raised the arm a little too high, but I didn't think the bone was broken.

I bathed the wounds, packed them with moss, and bandaged them as best I could with one hand. Soon the bleeding had stopped.

When I walked back up to the camp, Jack was gone. There was nothing unusual about that—he often took off for a few hours to catch something worth eating—but right then I wished he was close by, because I had to move, and move fast.

It was nearly dark, and that meant I'd been unconscious for quite a while. Curly and the others would have heard the shots, and most of them would even now be on my trail. I had to ride and keep on riding. I had to move fast, but not so fast my trail would be easy to follow. It was the only chance I had.

But even as I stepped into the saddle, a bullet cut through the air where I'd been only a second before. I stuck spurs to Buck and he leapt ahead. Other bullets cut the air around us, one clipping hair from Buck's mane. Then we were into the trees and running flat out.

Darkness fell and I had to slow Buck to a walk, but I kept going. In running from the men I'd headed south, so I stuck to that direction until I was too weary to stay in the saddle.

Not meaning to sleep, I stretched out on a bed of moss under a big tree. My shoulder and arm were throbbing, but sleep came almost the moment my head touched the ground. When I opened my eyes it was daylight.

Knowing I'd made a foolish mistake, I climbed back into the saddle and started moving again. Mountains loomed up ahead of us, and I had no idea where I was. Stopping briefly at a stream, I drank until I could hold no more, waited about five minutes, drank again.

Moving to high ground, I scanned the country behind us. I saw the riders almost at once. Three groups with four men in each group. The riders were twenty yards apart, and each group maybe three hundred yards from the next.

They were coming slow, and each man held a rifle. The center group was on my trail, while the outside groups would keep me from doubling back to get behind them.

But like I said, they were coming slow, not seeming in any hurry at all.

I pushed Buck away from them and rode hard for twenty minutes. Then I pulled up short. Those men were following along too slowly. It was like they knew I couldn't get away. They should have been in a hurry to catch me, but they weren't. That bothered me.

The mountains looming up before us weren't much as mountains go, but I could see a number of sheer granite cliffs. What I couldn't see was anything that looked like a pass.

That was it. That had to be it. Those men back there knew the country, and they knew I couldn't escape by riding south. Somewhere up ahead the mountains were going to stop me, and then they would move in for the kill.

I was hungry, but it was thirst that bothered me most of all. I drank my canteen empty and still my throat felt parched. And I was hot. A fever. I was getting a fever.

Stopping to refill my canteen, I drank again, then tried to ride west. No good. Four riders were there, not six hundred yards away, and they saw me. Rifles in hand, they angled to cut me off, forcing me back south. For an hour we played that game, and I came out the loser. The men were on three sides, and they were in no hurry.

Then I came out of the trees and found myself on a slope barren of anything except grass and rock. Three hundred yards ahead a steep cliff rose up, blocking me.

I couldn't go back and I couldn't go forward. Then a group of riders emerged from the trees at the west end of the clearing.

Buck responded when he felt my spurs, running right at the granite cliff. At the sheer base, I left the saddle, taking my canteen, rifle, and saddlebags.

Some force of nature had split a section of the cliff off, collapsing it into a jumble of jagged rock piled twenty feet deep at the base of the cliff. A thin trickle of water ran from the top of the cliff, splattering the rocks below. It seemed too puny to have worn away that much rock, but maybe in the past it had been much larger.

Scampering into the pile of rocks, I found a spot behind a two-thousand-pound slab of granite, eased my rifle over the top, and watched the riders come.

Unfortunately, they weren't stupid enough to charge straight in. Four men dismounted in the trees straight in front of me, four found cover at the west end of the clearing, and four at the east end. The clearing was perhaps six hundred yards long, running parallel to the face of the cliff. The way those men situated themselves, I had twelve men no more than three hundred yards from me, and that's easy range for a decent shot with a rifle.

Twelve rifles opened fire, and all I could do was duck my head and listen to the ugly sound of bullets ricocheting all around me.

After four or five shots each, they stopped shooting, and it became a waiting game—one I couldn't win.

Where was Charlie and the help he was supposed to bring? They were overdue. And where was Jack? He'd gone hunting before, but each time he'd always returned in a few hours' time.

There wasn't anyplace in that jumble of rocks for Buck, so when I left the saddle he went running back across the clearing and into the trees. Seemed like I was the only one stupid enough to get myself pinned down against that cliff.

My fever was getting worse, but there was little I could do for it except drink all the water I could hold. But if I had to drink anything, I wanted it to be coffee, so I gathered wood that had fallen from the top of the cliff over the years and built a small fire.

My coffeepot was still on Buck, but I had a tin cup in my saddlebags, and I made coffee in it, trickled a few drops of cold water in it to settle the grounds, and drank it, all those men be damned.

But I wasn't kidding myself. If my fever got worse, or if those boys out there were willing to lose a man or two in routing me out of the rocks, I wasn't going to get out of there alive.

By the time it was fully night, I was in more trouble than I'd ever seen. My fever was worsening, hunger was gnawing at my stomach like a rat, and I was getting weaker by the hour. In another day those men could simply walk up to the rocks and shoot me.

If there was any chance at all of escaping, it had to be while there was still enough strength in my body to move.

If only I could rest first, get even a little sleep, there might even be a chance to escape.

When night came, I moved about thirty yards along the rock fall, squeezed between two jagged boulders, sat down, and leaned back. It wasn't comfortable, but it didn't have to be. Sleep came before there was time to worry about how sharp the rocks were. And when I woke up I knew at once I'd slept too long, missed the last chance for escape I was likely to get.

A streak of daylight showed in the sky, though the sun hadn't yet made an appearance. My mouth and throat were dry, my lips rough. Water from the canteen helped my mouth and throat, but my mind didn't want to work, and nothing seemed capable of helping that.

I shook my head, tried to stand up. My whole body was stiff, and combined with my weakness, getting to my feet was a chore, but at last I made it. Something snapped beyond the rocks, as if a heavy man had stepped on a dry stick. Poking my head over the top to get a look was almost the last mistake I ever made.

All twelve men were coming, and they weren't thirty yards away. One of them fired and the bullet hit the boulder only inches from my face.

Rock dust nearly blinded me, but I moved, running down the jumble of rocks, trying to find a place where they couldn't get in behind me. A man loomed up before me and I fired my rifle from the hip. He staggered back, and as I ran by him I swung the rifle and caught him full in the face with the butt. He went down and stayed there.

Then they were all around me. A bullet took my leg from under me and I fell, still firing. Another bullet burned into my arm, and a third hit me somewhere low down. It sounded like a million rifles firing at once, and I knew I was dead. My rifle clicked on empty, but even as I grabbed for my Colt I realized that men were still falling, and their rifles were no longer aimed in my direction.

One of the men was facing almost directly away from me, looking down the barrel of his rifle. Then the top of his head seemed to explode. He fell, brain and blood staining the rock around him.

My vision was swimming and I had no idea what was happening or why. And I didn't care. Somehow, using my rifle for a crutch, I reached my feet. Through the spinning blur of my vision, men in pretty red uniforms charged across the clearing toward me, their rifles blazing.

I tried to take a step, fell, then crawled out of the rocks and into the clearing beyond. A man raised a rifle, aimed it at me, then was thrown backward like a rag doll as a hail of bullets struck him.

When again I tried to stand, something hairy and heavy knocked me down. A wet tongue licked at my face. The hand I reached to pat him was red with blood. "About time you showed up," I said. "I was beginning to wonder where you were."

It seemed that one minute I was lying there on the ground, trying to pet Jack, and the next minute I was lying in a bed with Charlie Slaughter leaning over me, his face only a couple of feet from mine.

CHAPTER 20

IN REALITY, THREE weeks had passed between the time I was shot and I awoke to see Charlie's face.

"Well, it looks like I'll have to pay your wages after all," Charlie said. "The doc said you were awake earlier, so I thought I'd come and see for myself."

If I'd been awake earlier, it was something I sure didn't remember. It took a minute to find my voice. "Wh . . . where am I?"

"Huh? Why, you're in Dawson, of course. You been here a couple of weeks. The rest of us just got in with the cattle yesterday, but they brought you on ahead."

I could remember nothing that happened after petting Jack. "How bad was I hit?"

The voice that answered came from the other side of the bed. Rolling my head that way, I saw a young man wearing a rumpled suit. His eyes were as red as his hair. "You weren't simply hit," he said, "You were shot to pieces. I took five bullets out of your hide, and patched three other places where bullets cut the skin or went on through. But aside from losing a lot of blood and getting a bit of infection, you were lucky. None of the bullets hit anything that could break, or anything you couldn't live without."

"Does that mean I'll live?"

"It means your wounds won't kill you. But something else will. You seem to be the kind of man who attracts trouble like a magnet, from all I hear."

"True enough," I said.

"Then I'd better stay in practice while you're in town. In the meantime, I need to check your wounds."

168

He ran Charlie out, but a pretty blond nurse came in to help with the bandages, and she had Charlie beat all hollow when it came to looks.

Charlie sold the herd without trouble, and the next day he came around with Billy. My right hand was about the only thing I had that wasn't bandaged, and Charlie stuck a thick envelope in it. "What's this?" I asked.

"It's your pay," Charlie said. "I put in the five hundred I borrowed, plus five thousand more. If that ain't enough, just say so."

"Five thousand! Charlie, you can't count. I figure I had about four hundred coming in wages. Not five thousand."

"You got coming what I say you got coming. Billy got the same, and you don't hear him complaining, do you?"

"No, but—"

"But nothing," Charlie said. "I made almost a hundred thousand dollars off that herd, but without you boys I'd be dead out there on the trail. I got enough money to see my daughter through the rest of her natural life, if I'm careful. So don't fuss with me, or I'll give you another five thousand."

I didn't fuss with him. Taking the money, I said thank you, and let it go at that.

I'd been laid up before, but never like for the length of time I was then. The doctor hadn't lied to me when he said I'd been lucky. The bullets chewed me up, but not one hit anything serious. Yet it takes time for muscle to heal, so it was several weeks before I could get out and look around Dawson.

By then winter was coming on strong, and I was wanting out. My body still wasn't up to a trip like that, however, and wouldn't be for several weeks.

Charlie was on the outside. Not knowing how his daughter was doing, or if she needed money, he took off for Skagway only a week after handing me the money. Billy was still around, and every few days we'd have a drink or a bite to eat together, but he'd staked a claim a ways down the line and couldn't leave it as often as he liked.

Billy had shown himself to be a man on the long drive, but now he looked the part. He'd put on muscle in his arms and shoulders, and he had a thick beard that made him look years older. By the time spring rolled around he'd be a full-fledged sourdough.

Jack was still with me, and not once in town did he make any trouble, partly because folks took one look at him and stepped aside. But then on a below-zero day sometime in January, I walked down to get a drink, Jack coming along as always.

The Monte Carlo was the finest place in Dawson, but though I'd gone there twice, I preferred a simpler place. McGreggor's Saloon was down on the waterfront and suited me fine. The men there knew Jack and they knew me. We all got along fine.

But the trouble with a gold town is people from all over come to it. I mean, you stay around a gold strike long enough, and you'll see everybody in the territory. So along with all the regulars that came into McGreggor's, every day brought in a few strangers from the cold.

On that particular day we hadn't much more than stepped through the door when a man I'd never seen before jumped up in front of me. "That's my dog," he said. "Where in hell did you find my dog?"

Jack took one look at the man and his hair stood right on end. His lips drew back and the fangs in his mouth looked like knives. "He sure don't act like your dog," somebody yelled.

"He's mine. I bought him in Skagway. He run away back in the summer."

"I've seen how you treat your dogs," another man said. "I don't blame him for running."

"That's my dog," the man said, "and I want him."

"I'd hate to get between a dog and his master," I said. "If he's your dog, lead him out of here."

The man reached for the fur on Jack's neck, thinking to drag him from the bar. Jack moved so fast it was hard to follow him. His jaws snapped down on the man's arm like a bear trap. Fortunately, the man was wearing a thick coat and all he lost was about six inches of leather. He jumped back, his face beet red.

Then he grabbed for a gun in his belt. My left arm and hand were still stiff, and my right leg hurt every time I walked anywhere. But my right hand and arm were fine. When he reached for that gun I snapped my Colt from the holster.

The sound of it cocking was loud in the stillness. The end of the barrel was pointed right between his eyes, and no more than six inches from the end of his nose. From that distance the hole in the end of that Colt must have looked like a cannon. That fellow swallowed hard, and his face drained of color.

"Mister," I said, "you said Jack was your dog. Jack says he isn't, and I believe him.

"He saved my life more than once out there, so I owe him. You, on the other hand, I don't owe a thing. Now, do you still claim he belongs to you?"

I hadn't shaved that morning, I had a wicked scar above my eye from the bullet wound, and he was looking at my face over the barrel of a Colt pointed his way. He didn't like what he saw. "N . . . n . . . no," he said. "I was wrong. G . . . g . . . guess he ain't my dog after all."

"Then you'd best get out of here and leave both of us alone."

"But, my food, I—"

"Get!"

He hit the door running, and he never looked back. I holstered my Colt. "Come on, Jack," I said. "Let's get something to eat."

In the winter, I learned, men fed their sled dogs frozen salmon. It was cheap, nourishing, and the dogs liked it. So I had a talk with McGreggor, and he went out and bought three hundred pounds of it. Jack had already eaten his way through a third of it and was working hard on the rest. I had a caribou steak, and Jack had the salmon. After a couple of bites, I was thinking of trading.

A man at a nearby table watched Jack eat five pounds of salmon in as many minutes and shook his head. "Mister," he said, "if your dog eats like that all the time, you'd have been better off to let that other fellow have him."

An old sourdough with a full white beard spoke up. "I know that other fellow," he said. "His name is George Baker, and he's a snake. He don't feed his dogs enough to keep a squirrel alive, then beats them when they get too weak to pull a heavy load. No, sir, that's one man who shouldn't be allowed to own a dog."

I'd been staying in a rented cabin not far from the waterfront, and after eating we walked back there. Snow was falling fast, and so was the thermometer. The waterfront was actually an ice front, and the only people coming up the river did so by dogsled.

But I wanted out. It was partly the cold that was getting to me, and partly the boredom. A man in a gold town who doesn't own a claim, or some kind of business, doesn't have many ways to kill time. After a time, even talking to friends gets tiresome, and some men turn to drinking the hours away.

That wasn't for me. Besides, it had been nearly a year since I'd seen Angie, and it would be several months more before I could get back to her. I wanted to know how she was and if Taminy Kisling had accomplished anything with Fergus Thornton. I doubted it, but I didn't know, and it was the not knowing that drove me crazy.

A year is a long, long time when two people are apart. Angie might even have forgotten me by now. If she was smart, she had found someone else. Angie deserved a man who wasn't on the run, a man who could give her a home, a family, and security.

Sitting there in my little cabin, listening to the howl of the wind, I realized why a lot of men drown their sorrows in a bottle of whiskey. I also realized how much I wanted out of Dawson.

The wicked part of winter was still ahead, and my body hadn't yet recovered from all the bullet holes, but I wanted out. Next morning I went looking for someone who was willing to make the trip and didn't mind having me tag along.

I found a man named Lynn Smith who was about to head downriver as far as Whitehorse, and he agreed to take me. "It isn't really too bad a trip," he said. "The only problem you'll have is getting over the Chilkoot."

"What about White Pass?" I asked. "That's how we came in."

"She's snowed-in solid," Lynn said. "Nobody can get through there either way, and won't till summer. But folks have probably scared you for nothing. The only reason people are afraid of the Chilkoot is because they usually have to make a dozen trips to get all their equipment across. If all you have is that dog, you'll make it without any trouble . . . if those wounds of yours are healed enough not to break open under stress."

"They're healed," I said. "I just haven't got all my strength back. The exercise will probably be good for me."

"Then we'll leave at dawn," he said. "Day after tomorrow. Of course this time of year dawn comes late, so you can sleep in."

We shook hands, and I went to buy myself some cold-weather gear. The sooner I got out of Dawson, the sooner I would see Angie again. I couldn't wait.

CHAPTER 21

WHEN WE STARTED downriver the temperature was right at seventeen below zero, a light snow was falling, and a stiff breeze was at our backs. Lynn's dog team was pure husky front to back, and the leader was a big gray-and-black named Colonel. He was leader of the pack, and he made the team of eight dogs behind him work as a unit.

In deep snow you don't ride a sled so much as you run along behind it, or sometimes in front to break a trail for the dogs, but the river had less than an inch of snow covering the ice in most places, and the going was easy. Dogs can pull a light sled faster than a man can run under those conditions, so I rode in the sled while Lynn rode the runner behind, his eyes locked on the river, looking for thin ice, or any other danger. Most of the time Jack ran along ahead of us.

It was something like two hundred and seventy or eighty miles to Whitehorse, but if the weather held up, we figured to make it in ten or twelve days. Three of the dogs in Lynn's string were new, however, and he wanted to work them slow for the first couple of days.

We made fifteen miles the first day, and twice I climbed out of the sled to run along behind, thinking to work myself back into shape. I couldn't have trotted more than a mile altogether, but by day's end I was done in.

We made camp in the shelter of some trees along the bank, and Lynn tied his dogs. Jack lay curled in the snow near the fire.

"I would tell you to tie him up," Lynn said, "but I can't

174

think of anything big enough to hurt him, unless he tangled with a bear."

I told Lynn about Jack's fight with the wolves. Lynn nodded. "Wolves kill most of their game by wearing it down, then hamstringing it. A wolf would kill the average dog without half trying, but I can see where Jack wouldn't worry much about them."

The moment Lynn finished speaking, a wolf howled somewhere in the night, and Jack's head came up. He darted off into the night, and Lynn watched him go.

"I'll tell you something else about wolves," he said. "A little over a year ago a fellow came up from the states. He was a professor at some fancy university back in New York, and he swore loud and long that wolves wouldn't attack a man.

"He said there wasn't a single documented case of it happening anywhere in North America, and all the stories were so much nonsense. He was always quoting from some book or the other, and said he intended to prove wolves were friendly toward man.

"Well, one day he put on this funny-looking red hat he liked to wear, stoked up his pipe, and went out looking for wolves."

"Did he prove his point?"

Lynn shrugged. "Nobody knows. He never came back. But every now and then some sourdough comes in from the bush and swears he saw a wolf wearing a red hat and smoking a pipe."

You get to know all about a man when you spend time on the trail with him, and over the next couple of days I learned quite a bit about Lynn Smith. He was from a small town in Indiana called New Castle, and he'd been in Alaska less than two years.

Newcomer or not, the Yukon Indians had already given him a name. They called him *Ooksook*, which means "too much grease."

"I was living in Anderson when I decided to come to the Klondike," he said. "They gave me quite a send-off, too. The Columbia Club had a fife-and-drum corps, and they marched me to the railroad station. My leaving was printed up in the paper, and half the girls in town were there to see me off.

"To tell the truth, after looking at some of those gals, I had half a mind not to leave. But I did, and I haven't regretted it for a minute."

Five days out we were hit by a snowstorm that slowly turned into a blizzard. When it reached the point where travel was impossible, we forted up and waited it out. It was almost four days before we dug ourselves out and pushed on to Whitehorse.

Where there had been only an inch or so of snow on the river ice before, there was now better than eighteen inches, though the wind was rapidly sweeping it toward shore.

We reached Whitehorse eight days later, and by then I was in much better shape than when I left Dawson. Running along behind the sled helped, and so did getting away from cities and people. I offered to pay Lynn for bringing Jack and me to Whitehorse, but he laughed it off.

"I had to come here anyway, Kerrigan, and I was glad for the company. You just go easy crossing the Chilkoot. That's quite a climb this time of year."

We shook hands and I went to find myself a warm room. The town was a major rest-and-resupply point for gold seekers coming in from the outside, and it was crowded. Most folks were coming in, but a few were going out, and I latched onto one group.

They weren't leaving for a couple of days, so I spent the time staying warm and eating the best food I could find. My second night in Whitehorse, I was sitting in a restaurant, sipping coffee after my meal, when a conversation at the next table caught my ear.

"Her name is Hannie Welch," a man was saying, "and

they say she's found a major strike. No telling how big it really is, but she's already sold two claims for fifty thousand each.

"I tell you, there's no justice in the world. I been up here for three years and ain't found the first nugget. Then along comes this fool of a woman, and she stumbles onto gold right off the bat."

I caught his eye. "Mister," I said, "Hannie Welch might be a lot of things, but a fool isn't one of them. She worked her way up here, and she went out alone into an area most men are afraid to think about. She found gold because she had guts and sense. And because she knew something you don't."

"Huh? What could she know that I don't?"

"That you can't find gold sitting in a nice, warm restaurant. Talking about gold doesn't mean a thing. You want it, you have to go get it."

The man's face was red and his lip was trembling in anger. Ignoring him, I payed my bill and left. The cold air felt good.

Looking out toward the wilderness north of town, I smiled. "Good for you, Hannie," I said. "Good for you."

Two days later, I left Whitehorse with nine other men. Three were sourdoughs who'd found a bit of gold and wanted to spend the rest of the winter in the warmer climate along the coast. The other six men were going out for more supplies and equipment. There was good money to be made hauling in gear for people, but it took a man with more muscle than sense to earn his living that way.

One look at the Chilkoot made me wonder if I shouldn't have waited for spring. Too late now. Putting one foot in front of the other, I started the long climb to the top.

It was well below zero, and three feet of snow covered the ground. Moving without snowshoes was almost impossible, though Jack seemed to manage all right, and a cold wind from the north filled the air with blowing snow that stung like needles against the skin.

In spite of this, Chilkoot Pass had men flocking over it by the hundreds. The call of gold was too strong to ignore, and men flocked to it, consequences be damned. They poured over the pass in all kinds of weather, in every season of the year, and they swarmed over the interior of the Yukon and spread across Alaska in search of a yellow metal that most couldn't even recognize by sight.

Not that I blamed them. Times were hard, and money was scarce. A man with a family has to make a dollar somehow, and this far north country offered a better chance than the cities back East.

The bullet wounds had taken more out of me than I realized. Three times on that climb I had to stop and rest, and the third time I nearly fell before I could sit. But at last we reached the top.

I was out of strength, completely exhausted, and dreaded the long descent to the bottom. I needn't have worried. Folks had to make that trip four times a day to get their gear across, and it didn't take people long to figure there was an easier way down the near side than on foot.

With little or no gear to carry, you could sit on a sled and have the ride of your life. Men sailed down that mountain on everything that would hold their weight on snow, and one fellow offered to let me ride his sled down.

It was a long sled, big enough for two or three men to sit on, but tired as I was, I had to think twice before accepting. "If you walk," he said, "it'll take you an hour. This thing will get us there in five minutes."

That made up my mind. I sat down on the sled behind him, and we started down the mountain. For the first thirty seconds we didn't gain much speed, then gravity took over and the wind began whipping at my face. The sled hit a pile of snow and we sailed about twenty feet, but somehow managed to remain aboard.

Jack was running along, trying to keep up, but after a minute we left him far behind. I don't know what speed we reached, but the long line of men forty yards to our right was a blur. Then we hit a bump. We both left the sled, rising high into the air. "Oh, noooooooooooo!" we both yelled.

When I came back down and hit that snow-covered mountain I was still traveling fast. If a man could plow dirt the way I plowed snow, he could give away his mules and still be the best farmer around. After somersaulting, sliding, and tumbling, I finally came to a stop not far from the bottom of the mountain. There was an acre of snow down my neck, and about that much more shoved up my pant legs.

My hat was gone, and had I stood still someone would have thought sure I was a snowman. Coughing, and trying to wipe snow from my eyes, I stood up. For a moment I couldn't see the other fellow, then he rose up from the snow.

"Whhoooeee!" he said. "You ready to climb back on?"

I politely declined his offer and walked the rest of the way down. Jack caught up with me near the bottom, and I looked back up the pass. It seemed a long, long way to the top. It had been quite a sled ride, at that.

Skagway had grown since I left it, but even in the winter it was crowded. I ate, found a hotel that didn't object to Jack—so long as I paid extra—then slept for twelve straight hours.

The first thing I did after waking up was walk down to Jeff's Place. I'd had enough trouble to last a lifetime, but Soapy Smith had cost Jamie Scott and Paul Donica their lives, and me a lot of grief. It was in me to make him answer for every last bit of it.

Jeff's Place was closed, but a hard-eyed man saw me trying the door. "Looking for someone?" he asked.

I turned to face the man. "I'm looking for Soapy Smith."

"You a friend of his?"

"Not hardly."

"Then it shouldn't bother you to know he's not around anymore. He had a shooting contest with a man named Frank Reid. They both lost. Soapy died on the spot, and Reid died later."

"You're wrong about one thing," I said. "It does bother me."

"Why's that?"

"Because I wanted to kill him myself."

I walked away, leaving the man standing there with a surprised look on his face.

I'd been in Skagway for three days before it occurred to me that Angie might have tried to write me a letter; she wouldn't have had an address, so she would have marked it for general delivery. I went down to the post office and asked if they had any letters for Clay Kerrigan. The short graying man behind the counter raised his eyebrows.

"That's like asking if Alaska has big bears. Hang on just a minute."

He went into a back room and came back out with seven letters. "Been coming in for months," he said. "I would have sent them back, but I figured you might be somewhere in the interior."

"I'm obliged to you," I said. "I haven't had news from the outside since I came here."

Taking the letters back to the hotel, I stretched out on the bed to read them. Five of the letters were from Angie, two from Taminy Kisling. I read Angie's first, in the order she sent them.

CHAPTER 22

ANGIE'S FIRST THREE letters were full of love and worry for me. Her fourth letter said that Taminy Kisling had a plan to stop Fergus Thornton. Without giving much detail, her fifth letter stated that Kisling had succeeded and Fergus had withdrawn the bounty on my head.

My head was spinning. Ripping open the first thick letter from Taminy, I read it all the way through, then read it again.

According to the letter, Taminy had set Fergus up by having a friend at a local newspaper run a story about my death at the hand of an assassin or assassins unknown. My death notice was also in the paper, along with details of my funeral.

Taminy then hired two Pinkerton agents, dressed them rough, and had them ride to Texas. They told Fergus they had killed me, and showed him my pocket watch as evidence. Fergus paid them the bounty on the spot.

With depositions from the two Pinkerton men, Fergus was arrested. That should have ended it, and perhaps it did, but it wasn't all cut-and-dried.

Texas was still the home of the big rancher, and Fergus had some powerful friends. It soon became obvious to Taminy that convicting Fergus in court would be difficult, so he tried something else.

Going to Texas himself, Taminy went to see Fergus and offered to drop the charges if he would agree to revoke the bounty on my head and place an ad to that effect in every major newspaper west of the Mississippi.

To Taminy's surprise, Fergus agreed to do just that.

Taminy was suspicious, but gave Fergus the chance to prove himself, and he did. The ads appeared just as promised.

I could have told Taminy how Fergus would react to being in jail. He would want out at all costs, and once out he would live up to his word.

But then I read Taminy's second letter. Being a good lawyer and a cautious man, he occasionally checked on Fergus Thornton. A month before Taminy wrote the second letter, Fergus and his sons disappeared. They simply vanished, and Taminy could learn nothing of their whereabouts.

"It worries me," the letter said.

> Deep in my being I always believed Fergus Thornton gave in too easily. He did not seem the kind of man who would allow himself to be defeated without a fight.
>
> Perhaps there is a logical reason for his disappearance that has nothing to do with you, Mr. Kerrigan, but I would not count on this being the case. My advice is for you to watch yourself. I believe you have not seen the last of Fergus Thornton.

It galled me, but I believed the same thing. Fergus Thornton wasn't the kind of man to quit easily. In fact, he wasn't the kind of man who would quit while he was still breathing.

Where was he, and why take his sons with him? Did Fergus know where I was now? If he had a man ride to Slater and ask around, he would certainly learn of Charlie's cattle drive to Alaska, and he might even learn that I had gone along.

But Alaska is a big, big place. Skagway is far from the only place where ships dock.

No, even if he knew I was in Alaska, he still had little chance of finding me. So what would he do? Where would he go?

I didn't know. I worried about it the way a dog worries over a bone, but after thinking myself silly, I simply had no idea.

It was my intention to catch the first ship out of Skagway when spring came, but the wait was a long one. Spring came at last, and it came so suddenly that it caught me off guard. One day it was well below freezing and the land was covered with snow, and the next day it was seventy degrees and the only color to be seen across the land was green. (I suppose the change didn't really occur that fast, but it seemed to, and I was glad for it.)

I booked passage out on a steamship, and sat back to wait for the departure just two days away. But the day after I bought my ticket, I was down at the dock watching another ship coming in, and there on the deck, her blond hair blowing in the wind, stood Angie Douglas.

Not many things in life have shaken me, but seeing her did. Our eyes met, and I suddenly felt so dizzy I had to grab something to keep from falling. She was the first one off the ship, and when she came into my arms it was like heaven come to earth. Every care I had in the world vanished.

A long time later she leaned back enough to look me in the eye and I said, "Angie, I can't believe this. I've got to be dreaming. But if I am, I don't want to wake up."

"It's really me," she said. "I . . . I had to come. You didn't answer my letters, and when Charlie got back he told us you had been shot. He said you were going to be fine, but when he told us how bad it was . . . I had to come, Clay. I had to."

"It's all right, Angie. I'm glad you came. Holding you in my arms like this makes up for everything I've—"

As I spoke, a movement on the deck behind Angie caught my eye. Looking toward it I saw three men standing there. Angie felt my muscles go tight, and she followed my eyes.

"Oh, that's Mr. Walker," she said. "We met on the ship. He seems very nice."

"His name isn't Walker," I said. "It's Thornton. That old man is Fergus Thornton, and those other two are his sons."

"What? I don't understand. He said—"

Large crates and other cargo lined the docks, and I gently pushed Angie behind a stack of boxes. "Stay there," I said. "Don't come out until it's over."

Angie's face showed fear and confusion, but to her credit she did as I asked.

Never taking his eyes off mine, Fergus walked down off the boat, Trace and Daniel flanking him. They stopped thirty feet away. There must have been fifty men near us, but they were men who knew when trouble was coming. They saw us square off, saw how our hands hovered close to our Colts, and they scattered for cover. In seconds there wasn't anyone nearby except for me and the Thorntons.

"You've led us a good chase, Kerrigan," Fergus said, "but the trail has come to an end."

"This doesn't have to happen," I said. "It isn't too late to back away."

Trace was sweating, and I knew he didn't want to be a part of killing anyone. He might draw, and he might shoot, but he didn't want it. Fergus stood between his sons like an oak between two saplings. He would take a lot of killing.

I'd never seen Daniel draw, but Trace had said he was fast, and he carried himself like a man who knew how to use a Colt. He stood next to Fergus, and he was the calmest one of the three. When the shooting started, Daniel had to be my first target.

"You killed two of my sons, Kerrigan," Fergus said. "Two, damn you! You have to die for that."

Without warning, Fergus drew. The moment his hand closed around the butt of his Colt, I drew and fired, not at Fergus, but at Daniel. It was a good thing.

I actually started my draw the tiniest fraction of a second

before Daniel started his, but his pistol was coming in line when I fired. If I'd shot at Fergus, I'd be dead.

As it was I fired a shade too quick and my bullet caught Daniel in the left leg. He went down, losing his Colt in the fall. Fergus fired just as I dived behind a big steam engine, and his bullet whiffed past my ear, sounding like an angry bee, but doing no harm.

Then I was safely behind the steam engine. Two more bullets clanged off the metal. Trace was yelling, "Stop it, Pa. Stop it. Daniel needs help. God, look how he's bleeding."

Risking a glance around the steam engine, I saw Daniel lying on the dock, Trace bent over him. There was blood everywhere. Daniel's face was white, and Trace looked scared. Fergus snapped a shot at me, missed by inches.

"Damn it, Fergus," I yelled. "Put away that gun and help your son. My bullet must have hit an artery. He's bleeding to death."

"He'll be all right. As soon as I kill you, I'll get him to a doctor. Damn you, Kerrigan. Show yourself."

Risking another look, I saw that Daniel was now flat on the dock. A big puncture wound in the artery can bleed a man dry in minutes. My heart was racing.

"I'm coming out, Fergus," I yelled. "You might be able to watch him die, but I can't."

Taking a breath, I holstered my Colt and stepped from behind the engine. Fergus raised his Colt, and at that instant Trace stood up and jumped between us, facing his father. His Colt was in his hand, and it was pointed at Fergus.

"That's enough, Pa," he said. "Kerrigan didn't kill Roland or Jesse. You did, Pa. You could've stopped Roland from drawing on Kerrigan. And it was because of you that Jesse died. Now you're letting Daniel bleed to death."

Fergus looked like a ghost, and his voice was choked. "You . . . you'd shoot me? You'd shoot your own father?"

Trace was crying. The Colt in his hand slowly lowered. "No. No! But you've got to stop this, Pa. How many of us have to die before you stop?"

I was already beside Daniel. I jerked his belt free and put it around his leg above the wound, pulling it as tight as I could. The bleeding slowed, but didn't quite stop.

"Help me carry him," I yelled to Trace. "If we don't get him to a doctor he's going to die."

Trace holstered his gun and ran over. He lifted Daniel by the arm and leg on his side, while I did the same. The Colt still in Fergus Thornton's hand twitched. "Shoot and be damned," I said. "Or put that thing away and help us."

For a moment more Fergus hesitated, then he shoved the Colt back in its holster. He came over to us, put his hands in to replace the grip Trace had. "I can carry him," he said to me. "Show me where the doctor is."

I'd been in Skagway long enough to learn where just about everything was. I hadn't seen Jonas Carlyle since helping him find his medical supplies a year earlier, but I did know where his office was, and I led Fergus there.

Doctor Carlyle went to work on Daniel at once, but his eyes met mine. "Don't I know you?" he asked.

"Uh-huh. I helped you find some things on the dock about a year ago."

"Oh, of course. I do remember you. Who put the bullet in this young man's leg?"

"I did."

"Oh, I see."

He worked rapidly on the leg, and he worked well. Twenty minutes later he put in a last stitch and looked at Fergus. "Are you his father?"

"I am."

"Well, he'll live. But if you'd gotten him here just five minutes later he wouldn't have. I don't know what went on out there, but he's a very lucky young man."

Fergus Thornton looked old, haggard, worn out. The

bull of the woods was gone, and a tired old man was in his place. He met my eyes, started to say something, then lowered his eyes and walked out of the office.

"He'll be all right," Trace said. "Thank you, Kerrigan. You didn't have to help Daniel."

"Yes, I did. Some things you have to do no matter what. Helping him was one of them."

Angie had been waiting outside, and I went to join her. Taking her in my arms, I looked into those sky-blue eyes. "It's all over," I said. "Tomorrow we can go home."

"Good," she said. "But there's something I want to do first."

"What's that?"

"I want to get married," she said. "I want you and me to find the nearest preacher, and I want to get married."

I smiled. "Yes, ma'am," I said. "Yes, ma'am."

If you have enjoyed this book and would like to receive details on other Walker Western titles, please write to:

Western Editor
Walker and Company
720 Fifth Avenue
New York, NY 10019